UNICORN SEEKERS

ISBN 978 0702 30696 9

A CIP catalogue record for this book
is available from the British Library.

Printed by CPI Group (UK) Ltd, Croydon, CR0 4YY
Paper made from wood grown in sustainable forests
and other controlled sources.

1 3 5 7 9 10 8 6 4 2

www.scholastic.co.uk

UNICORN SEEKERS

THE MAP OF LOST UNICORNS

CERRIE BURNELL

SCHOLASTIC

For Amelie and all her friends, who have
found magic in Crystal Palace Park.

From the diary of Araminta Lang

May 21st 1918, Rome, Italy

For as long as there have been dreams and thunder, there have been unicorns.

I know from the many journeys I have been on, and from the gifted seekers I've met along the way, that it was a child who first dreamed of a unicorn, long, long ago, in the time of hurricanes and floods, darkness and courage. It was a time when people and horses lived in harmony.

The night the first unicorn came into being, a terrible tempest swept across the land, frightening folk into forests and caves.

In the furthest-flung corners of the world, nine fearless children were lost among mountain peaks, deep valleys and swirling shorelines, with nothing to protect them but their horses. The world grew dark and dangerous, rain lashed down and a howling wind shrieked through the sky. The horses stepped forward to protect the children and, at that very moment, a wishing star fell from the clouds, splintering into nine gleaming pieces.

Each of the children wished with all the love in their young beating hearts that their horses would not be harmed by the storm. And, when lightning struck, each horse was marked for ever with a horn made of bone and starlight, and enchanted with the power of thunder.

"Storm Horses", as they were then known, have lived by our side ever since. Basking on the banks of lakes at midnight, cantering through deserts of shining sands, racing through the waves of deep oceans and dancing in the light of a million dazzling moons. For unicorns, being born of storms and starlight, are of course nocturnal.

But the world has changed so much since the Night of the Wishing Star, and somewhere along the way, people lost their belief in magic. And so unicorns have become invisible to us.

They are still here, of course, but mostly they appear in our dreams, and we awaken feeling touched by hope or the ability to see things more clearly.

Although, there are a few rare and very special people who can still see unicorns. Some never realize they have their gift, and simply wander through the world with a quiet belief in enchantment — a feeling that there is more to the world than what's in front of them. Others are lucky enough to glimpse a unicorn in childhood and never stop searching. Some, like myself, discover their talent much later in life and are ever grateful for its wonder.

These people — mostly children — are called Unicorn Seekers. And if you are reading this entry in my journal, there is a chance that you are one too.

CHAPTER ONE
THE FEATHER AND FERN

In the vast city of London – where the sky can turn from the brightest blue to a gold-tinged grey in the blink of a dreamer's eye – just south of the great misty river that runs through the city's bustling heart, and close to a lovely leafy park, lived a girl named Elodie Lightfoot.

Each morning, sunlight streamed through the tall windows of the second-floor flat where Elodie lived with her dad (and sometimes her mum – Maman – who was often away working for a famous fashion house in Paris). On this particular morning, Elodie blinked open her sleepy brown eyes, rolled out of bed, and picked up her bright pink brush.

Her hair, which she got from her maman, was a halo of spiralling ringlets that tumbled and danced around her face. Elodie loved each curl as fondly as a tree loves its leaves, but brushing it wasn't always easy. Frowning, Elodie put the brush back down on top of her overcrowded bookcase and slowly began to get ready for school. But her mind drifted off into sun-warmed daydreams of all the new tricks she was going to perfect on her roller skates, and the delicious flavours of jam she would try with her croissants.

"Six minutes till we leave, Elle. You almost ready?" came her dad's lively voice.

Elodie was startled back to reality. Was it that time already?

Elodie's dad, Max, ran the Feather and Fern coffee van in the lovely, leafy park just across the road from their flat. Every day he rose six minutes after sunrise and began loading almond butter croissants into the oven, adding sugarless icing to the oatmeal cookies and preparing gluten-free treats and fluffy pains au chocolat for all of South London.

It was all a well-timed art, which meant Elodie and her dad had to leave the flat exactly an hour later. Elodie glanced at the moon dial clock on her bedroom wall. Six minutes to go and she was nowhere near ready!

She twirled around the room in a mild panic, seizing a violet-coloured scrunchie and attempting to squeeze her hair into a high bun, but a handful of curls pinged out. Elodie gave up, flopping on to her bed in defeat.

It was moments like this when she missed her maman the most.

Not just because Maman was a hero at rescuing hairstyles and had a way of never panicking, even if they were running late. Elodie simply missed her. The sound of her singing in the kitchen, the scent of her skin (which always smelled of Parfum de Rose), the lightness of her laugh.

"I'm sorry, Maman," she whispered, leaping up suddenly and grabbing a little rusted silver tub from the back of her overcrowded bookcase.

This was her maman's trusted lotion. Quite where

it came from, nobody knew, but it had once belonged to Elodie's great-grandmother, Elise de Lyon. Elodie was not really supposed to use the "magic lotion" as she had called it when she was little. Her maman had told her so. But time was ticking by quick as lightning, and she could not make her dad late for work again!

The pot was the colour of rust and silver and seemed centuries old. It had a mythical winged horse imprinted upon its lid, and was so tightly closed that it took all of Elodie's effort to unscrew it. The scent when she finally managed to do so was so wonderful that a single breath of it made Elodie feel full of hope.

At first, the entire room filled with the aroma of rain on a midsummer eve, then came the rushing saltiness of the sea, followed by the swift scent of frost. And there was something else Elodie couldn't quite place... The smell of moonlight? She was never sure.

Elodie closed her bright hazelnut eyes, letting the scent carry her away. She felt touched by a warm golden glow as the sounds outside her bedroom window hushed, and the only rhythm was that of her heart: slow and steady, like the pounding hooves of a horse.

Did her heart quicken? For the beating seemed to get faster, as if something swift and graceful was racing towards her.

"Elle?"

Elodie blinked and stared at the moon dial clock in panic, but the clock's hands had hardly ticked on.

"Almost ready, Dad," she yelled, scooping the tiniest amount of "magic lotion" from the jar and running it rapidly through her curls.

The lotion was always cold to the touch, as if it held the memory of snow, but it warmed in her hands like honey. It seemed the moment it touched Elodie's hair, her tangles became tendrils that glistened and gleamed and did exactly what she wanted them to do. Perhaps it was just the scent that made her feel closer to Maman, and she remembered how much she actually loved her wondrous curls. Grinning with joy, she twisted her hair up, closed the precious antique tub and slid it back on to the bookcase. Then she grabbed her school bag, slung her rainbow-laced roller skates over her shoulder and hurried into the sourdough-scented kitchen to help her dad carry everything to the van.

Down the creaky stairs they crept with armfuls of freshly baked baguettes, jars of pickled ginger and shiny fruit jam, baskets of buttery warm croissants, boxes of berry biscuits, stacks of sultana and cinnamon buns, and flasks of almond and coconut milk.

Elodie held her breath as they tiptoed past the Singhs' flat on the first floor, hoping that they didn't wake lovely old Mrs Singh, who was eighty-six! Clasping a basket of buns, she leaned on the bright blue front door so it swung open into a June morning of sunshine and birdsong.

"Perfect weather for croissants," her dad announced.

Elodie rolled her eyes. "You say that every morning," she sighed as they crossed their almost empty road and slipped through the slightly rusted park gate, unseen by anyone but the Singhs' vicious one-eyed cat, Pirate.

Elodie loved this time of morning, when everything felt possible. The boating lake was every colour of autumn, dew sparkled upon the tiny wildflowers, and in the soft, early light Elodie could almost imagine that the ancient statues scattered throughout the park were real.

The Feather and Fern coffee van was parked just beyond the lake, beneath two weathered and wise-looking oak trees. The van was very vegan and prided itself on selling the best plant-based delights south of the misty river. To reflect this, Max had painted the van bright green, like the feathers of the parakeets that lived in the oak trees. Elodie and her best friends had decorated it with a forest of colourful ironwork sculptures of tropical leaves and flowers.

Elodie put down her baskets and boxes and opened the hatch of the van as the smell of brewing coffee filled the air.

The sound of wheels whirring over gravel made Elodie turn, her heart dancing as she waved to a girl with bright indigo braids and glossy leopard-print roller skates.

"Dad, I'm going to skate with Marnie-Mae," she called, already kicking off her school shoes and pushing her feet into her well-worn skates. They had once been strawberry pink, but sunshine and dust had faded them to a dusky mauve.

Elodie half-hopped, half-glided over a little bank of daisies and on to the park's main pathway, where Marnie was circling her mum, Joni.

"I'll see you at six, Marnie. Thanks for getting them to school, Max!" called Joni, giving Marnie and Elodie swift kisses before darting away to catch a train into the city.

"Race you!" cried Marnie-Mae, shooting off before Elodie had even finished fastening her rainbow laces. She bound them into a triple loop, though it didn't really matter what clever thing Elodie did with her skates – Marnie was always faster. Years of ballet and karate had given her excellent balance and fearless speed.

But where Marnie was fast, Elodie, like her name, was light-footed and nimble.

As she took off after her friend, Elodie couldn't help but laugh out loud. Roller-skating always made her feel invincible. Zooming over the path, she caught up with Marnie halfway along, and they high-fived each other in a soaring circle.

Something caught Elodie's eye and she stumbled to a stop, nearly falling and crashing into Marnie-Mae, who swept her into a hug.

"Sorry, sorry," Elodie said, regaining her balance. She peered around in slight confusion. "I thought I saw . . . a horse? Like a pony, or maybe a deer."

"What?" shouted Marnie-Mae, whizzing around her. "It was probably just Rufus, silly!"

They turned then, together, both sliding in a half moon, like two halves of a heart, and met at the point in the middle, gazing together at an enormous, slow St Bernard dog that was lolling towards them, its tongue hanging out as it ambled along with their friends Kit and Caleb.

Kit and Caleb were homeschooled, something Elodie was super jealous of. To spend her days learning maths by gathering conkers, or studying geography by following a compass through the park's maze, or admiring the stars by the lake at twilight sounded like a dream.

As Marnie flew off to hug Rufus, Elodie glanced back over her shoulder.

She was certain she had seen a dark, beautiful horse step out of the shadows. For a moment it had seemed clear as a star. But behind her there was only the wide, sweeping park, with its swooping parakeets and early morning joggers – its lake of browns and golds resting perfectly still, and its strange, unblinking statues.

"Hey!" Elodie grinned as they all launched into an accidental race, with Rufus plodding breathlessly behind.

"What are you two up to today?" asked Marnie-Mae.

"Field school and lake study in the morning," called Kit, shooting away from them. "Then Spanish this afternoon." Marnie wrinkled her nose. "I'm not so keen on Spanish – I want to learn Chinese."

Elodie shrugged. French was the only language she knew. And a few of her dad's Gaelic songs.

"You know when you do field school in the park?" she asked, sliding to a stop beside one of the many oak park benches just as Kit attempted to jump over it.

"Yeah?" he answered absent-mindedly.

"Have you ever seen a horse?"

Kit lost his balance and crashed to his knees, Marnie glided over and helped him up.

"No. I've never seen a horse, but Caleb has. He's always going on about it."

They all gazed at Caleb, who was perched on the bench opposite, lining up acorns as Rufus dozed contentedly by his feet. Caleb, who was autistic, wasn't really into conversation, but he could talk for hours about nature and wildlife and things that he loved. He knew everything about every type of tree in the park. And everything about all the water birds that lived on the lake. And he could name every famous YouTube skater.

Elodie skated over and crouched down to stroke Rufus.

"Have you ever seen a horse in this park?" she asked.

Caleb frowned, then shook his head. "Not a horse. I've seen a unicorn."

Elodie smiled at him as she stood up. "I would love to see a unicorn," she said.

"It's black, but also blue – like midnight," said Caleb. "And it looks like a horse at first, but when it steps into moonlight, you can see its deadly horn."

Elodie stared at Caleb for a long moment, until her dad's voice carried through the trees.

"Elle, Marnie, time for school!"

"We've got to go," they said in unison, grasping each other's hands and zipping off towards the Feather and Fern.

CHAPTER TWO

TWILIGHT IN LONDON

School rushed by in a whirlwind of lessons, and then Marnie had swimming at the sports centre while Elodie had gymnastics. They met up afterwards, as they did every Wednesday, to dance on their skates, up and down the wide concrete expanse outside the sports centre. It was the only time they got to really practise their backwards gliding.

"Look at you two superstars," called Joni, strolling towards them. Marnie-Mae flew into her mum's arms and Elodie paused to wave.

The only time she ever longed for her life to be more like Marnie's was in moments like this, when Marnie-Mae's mum got back from the ColourPop lipstick company and the two of them went home together. Sometimes Elodie missed Maman so sharply it ached.

"See you tomorrow, Elle!" Marnie and her mum chimed before heading off towards their home.

"See you," Elodie waved, skating back to her dad and deciding to take the longer route as it was not yet sunset and the evening breeze was bursting with the scents of summer. Skidding and scuttling along the gravel track, Elodie skated past the patch where a palace of crystal had once stood. Home to the silent princess – Princess Grace – it had burned down hundreds of years ago, but you could still see the remains of its grandeur.

She looped past the maze and the deserted stage, then flew down the main walkway towards the Feather and Fern, smiling at her dad who was still busily serving customers. The light was beginning to fade a little, but the park still hummed with life, so Elodie leaned into the breeze and skated a lap of the lake, passing the oddly shaped dinosaur statues that circled it. They were huge! Some of them comical, others regal, and they gave the park a surreal feeling of enchantment.

There were other statues of stags and woodland

animals that were more hidden amongst the trees. One that had just been repainted caught Elodie's eye. It was a graceful deep-black horse. Or was it the darkest blue, like the colour of the sky around the edge of a star?

Elodie put her stopper down, abruptly spinning in a half-circle as she braked to gaze at the horse.

It was perfectly still. *It must be new,* she thought, feeling drawn to it. But as she stared, the horse's coat seemed to almost ripple and its eyes somehow glistened, as if they held a sparkling light. Its mane and tail looked as glossy as silk.

It's black but also blue, just like midnight.

Elodie frowned. Had Caleb meant this statue? It did look more real than any of the others. *Maybe Caleb made a mistake?* she thought, as wind whistled through the leaves, making her shiver. For a single moment, Elodie was *sure* she saw a horn – pale as glass and glimmering in the brightest silver – on the magnificent horse's forehead.

But then the wind stopped, and the statue was just a strikingly graceful horse once more.

Shaking her head, Elodie skated on. Over the little

bridge and around an island of wild heather and day lilies she went, and as the Feather and Fern came back into sight, she glanced back to catch sight of the lovely dark horse again and nearly tripped in surprise.

The horse wasn't there.

Elodie stumbled.

"Where's the midnight horse?" she murmured, and she startled when a familiar voice answered her.

"It goes back to the gate at twilight."

Elodie whipped around to see Caleb and Rufus lounging on a lakeside bench. Rufus was chewing a large stick and Caleb was sketching a family of coots in charcoal.

Elodie skated over and perched beside the great shaggy dog.

"Which gate, Caleb?" she asked, trying to keep her voice steady.

"The secret gate that no one uses."

Elodie closed her eyes, trying to picture every single entrance to the park. There were so many – she had no idea which one might be secret.

"Can you show me?" she asked.

"No. Not today – I'm drawing," Caleb answered,

not taking his eyes from the page.

"OK, well maybe tomorrow?" Elodie asked. Her head was completely spinning, but for now her dad was waiting. She zoomed off to find him.

"Dad, is there a secret gate to the park?" she asked later as they delivered leftover biscuits and vegan pastries to the Singhs.

"Not that I can think of," said her dad with a shrug. But he paused on the stairs, glancing back at her as Pirate the cat hissed at them crossly.

"There are two gates at the very top, near the station. One leads to the sports centre, the other is called Rainbow Gate and leads straight to the end of the rainbow."

"Dad!" Elodie sighed. "I'm *serious*."

Yet when supper had been eaten, the dishes had been washed and the flat had fallen into a slumbering silence, Elodie found she could picture the Rainbow Gate quite clearly. As if she had known of it all along and just needed to be reminded. And, in the depths of her mind, bathed in sparkling silver light at the gate's entrance, stood a horse of midnight and mystery. A horse with an icicle-sharp horn.

Notes from the Arctic Circle
Manuscript by Byron Bjornson

March 2nd 1916

A most astonishing discovery!

The creatures I have been tracking are not a herd of arctic horses, as I first believed.

They are too strange. Too ... luminous. Untouched by frost or storms. In certain lights they appear to have horns, like that of a rhino but clear as ice or even starlight. They are wild but intelligent, and are able to swim beneath the water's surface for long periods of time.

In my life, I have never witnessed anything so extraordinary.

They can only be described as creatures of folklore, known throughout legendary texts as unicorns. I can hardly believe it! The entire purpose of my expedition has altered, for, rather than studying the great white bear, I will now devote my energies to understanding these superb beings.

But how peculiar that I came across them quite by chance, on a pale arctic night, when the sky was still bright as day even though it was midnight. A helpful boy from the fishing village pointed one out to me. He called it a "storm horse".

Since my first introduction I have been drawn to them: observing that they mostly eat violet thistles and, surprisingly, moths; tracking them as they roam with grace in deep water and over ice. Though, mostly I see them at night (could they be nocturnal?). They seem to have an affinity with moonlight.

It has been impossible to discover where they slumber or rest. Either these clever creatures know how to hide, or they can camouflage themselves entirely in the snow. Though, I do find myself wondering if they are able to somehow pass through a gateway unseen by the human eye, disappearing from our view. For, sometimes, in the few sacred moments just as darkness falls and the sky turns grey, while the northern lights gleam their beauty, these wonderful storm horses appear to vanish, as if into a void.

I will make it my life's work to discover where they go. What an honour it will be!

What an–

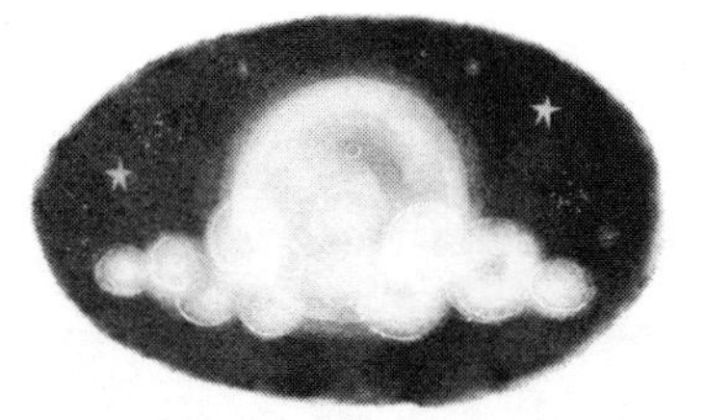

CHAPTER THREE

A DREAM OF MIDNIGHT HORSES

Something woke Elodie, and she sat up. Her heart was racing too quickly.

Moonlight, silvery and soft, flooded into her bedroom from where she had fallen asleep with the curtains open. The moon dial clock said seven minutes past midnight, and it seemed to be ticking much louder than usual. Elodie shivered. Why was the room so cold? She hopped out of bed to grab her polka-dot dressing gown, glancing down at the deserted street. The pavements were dappled in lamplight and a pattern of leafy shadows.

Something stirred and Elodie pressed her face up against the glass, hoping to glimpse a city fox. The tick of the clock got louder. Or was it the beat of her heart? Then she heard a pounding rhythm that seemed to whisper of fearless journeys and star-struck skies. It sounded like horse hooves.

Elodie gasped as the sound of cantering echoed through the stillness and a horse broke from the shadows, galloping down the middle of her sleepy street. It was the horse statue she had seen earlier – she was sure of it. But now it was most definitely alive.

The horse halted beneath Elodie's window, rising up superbly on to its hind legs, its front hooves kicking so powerfully that they seemed to churn up the air. It was looking directly at her.

Elodie's eyes opened wide as she gazed deeply into the horse's. The horse's eyes were dazzling. The clouds shuddered, thunder rumbled and a downpour of wild summer rain began to tumble from the sky. But as the clouds parted, a single beam of moonlight split the night like lightning. In its swift, pure glare, Elodie saw the unmistakable gleam of a unicorn's horn, right between the horse's ears.

It was luminous as the ice beneath the northern lights, sharp as the blade of a dagger carved from bone, and lovely as the first note of a songbird at

dawn. It was, Elodie thought, like looking at a miracle. She opened her mouth to speak, to call out through the window and the lashing rain. She wanted to say, "*I see you. I believe in you. I know you.*"

But the screech of wheels cut through the storm, and the headlights of a car glared through the night. The unicorn bolted, galloping into a bank of shadows and nimbly vaulting the park fence, disappearing amongst the inky trees. With a heave, Elodie pushed open her sash window and leaned out into the downpour.

But the unicorn was gone.

The street was eerily calm, except for the fast-falling rain and the lone car, which was a rich cherry-red. It had slowed right down to a crawl, inching its way past the park. Elodie withdrew into her room so the driver wouldn't see her, and hid behind the billowing velveteen curtain. It didn't look like one of her neighbours' cars, and it gave Elodie a bad feeling in her stomach.

The car came to a stop, and an alarmingly chic woman in a long, sweeping black mac and towering stilettos stepped out. She arranged her rather fabulous hat over her bobbed hair, then produced what looked like an extra-large magnifying glass and proceeded to search for something on the road.

From behind the curtain, Elodie squinted through the rainy dark. She could see nothing on the road but puddles. The woman squatted down and, to Elodie's surprise, appeared to sniff the pavement. Then she rose sharply, opened her lips and tasted the rain.

"It was here. For certain," she said in a clipped accent Elodie knew to be Parisian. "Next time we must be faster!" the woman snapped, folding herself into the car as it pulled away. Elodie peered after it in bewilderment.

As the car rolled down the street, a beautiful but forlorn face with large, sad eyes gazed out of its back window. Elodie's heart lurched. Could it really be her?

"Maman?" she breathed, but the car had vanished into the night, just like the unicorn.

The next morning, Elodie was up at six minutes past sunrise, obediently helping her dad with all of the baking, icing and steaming so they could set off for the Feather and Fern early – for once in their lives!

"Dad, I had such a vivid dream last night," Elodie said as they crept past the

Singhs', and she secretly fed a handful of crumbs to Pirate.

"It started with thunder. Then there was this magnificent..." She paused, about to say the word *unicorn*, but instead found herself saying, "Storm horse."

Her dad stopped mid-stride and turned to stare at her, his expression soft with concern.

"It stopped underneath my window, then it leapt the fence to the park and vanished."

Elodie's dad chuckled warmly, as if he were relieved, and turned his face to the sky, assessing the weather as he did every morning before announcing, "It's the perfect weather for croissants."

"But that's not all, Dad, there was this car and—"

"Morning, Max!" A bubbly, breathless voice cut across Elodie, completely interrupting their conversation. Sophia – Kit and Caleb's frazzled-looking mum – jogged over, with the boys a little way behind her and Rufus on a lead. She appeared to be trying to get Rufus to leave the park. Rufus appeared to be refusing.

"Morning." Max nodded cheerfully.

"I've got to take Rufus to get his teeth cleaned. Caleb's upset about it and doesn't want to come. It's always very noisy at the vets and the lights are a bit too bright for him. Could you keep an eye on the boys for me? They can skate with Elle and Marnie, and I should be back by eight to take them to violin."

"He would love to!" cried Elodie before her dad could answer. "We can start with a loop of the lake. I'll make sure we're back to help open," she beamed, giving her dad a hug.

Then she was flying over the daisies, shoes tumbling off in the grass, skates sliding on, rainbow laces knotting almost automatically into splendid bows.

"Race you to the dinosaurs!" Elodie shrieked and the three of them took off in an arc of grit and fallen petals. Their wheels whipped up dust as they tore around the lake, startling the Canada geese and red-eyed ducks.

When they reached the dinosaur statues, Elodie cheekily changed the rules. "First one to the top of the park gets a blueberry muffin!" she chanted, lancing off uphill. The boys tailed her, huffing and puffing and trying not to laugh.

Skating uphill was never easy, but it was a challenge they all adored: imagining that they were running up a wall of ice. You had to *believe* you could do it in your heart, then power on until you made your dream come true. Caleb won, leaving Kit and Elodie panting behind him. Elodie leaned up against a huge gnarled wild cherry tree, catching her breath as she handed over the muffin.

"I saw the black horse again last night, in a dream, I think," she said, quietly.

"You mean the midnight unicorn," Caleb corrected her.

Elodie nodded, and Kit frowned but didn't interrupt them. He was studying his brother closely. Kit always knew when Caleb was making something up, telling one of his epic fantastical stories or fibbing to try and keep out of trouble. But Caleb's face was completely serious.

"Where does the midnight unicorn go at night?" asked Elodie. "You said something about a gate?"

"Right there," Caleb said, pointing away from the main gate to a run-down track. Over its entrance hung a ramshackle sign that said, "Rainbow Gate".

Elodie skated over, laying her hands upon the gates to give them a gentle push. They swung open slowly. She took a deep breath, crossed her fingers and skated through.

Nothing happened. The blue skies were still summery and warm, the green parakeets were still calling and there was no sign of a unicorn or even a horse. Elodie smiled to cover her disappointment.

Kit and Caleb roller-skated over, and, as they headed along the slightly windy track, she told them of her strange dream. Caleb listened very closely. He was incredibly quiet, dropping crumbs of muffin behind him as they skated.

"And it was the same horse that you thought was a statue?" asked Kit.

"Yes," Elodie insisted. "The same horse – unicorn – that Caleb can see."

"But why can no one else see it?" asked Kit, who preferred to find a logical explanation for everything.

"You can. It's right there," said Caleb.

Elodie and Kit almost collided as they both turned abruptly to find a breathtakingly beautiful black horse standing right behind them, happily munching muffin crumbs. Elodie gasped. It was huge, so much bigger than in her dream.

"That's definitely a horse," Kit whispered, not wanting to alarm the graceful beast as he held out a dandelion for it to nibble.

"It must pretend to be a horse in the daytime," said

Caleb thoughtfully, as if he were working it all out. "But at twilight, it becomes a unicorn."

The horse looked up, as if to agree, and shook its silky mane. Elodie sucked in her breath sharply. For, as the air glimmered and trembled, sunlight seemed to catch on the almost visible point of a dagger-sharp horn.

CHAPTER FOUR

A UNICORN IN THE PARK

"Kit, move back!" Elodie urged, trying not to alarm her friend.

"Why?" said Kit, frowning. He was clearly quite taken by the majesty of the horse.

"In case you get struck by the horn," answered Caleb, easing forward and gently leaning against the animal's nose as if they were the greatest of friends.

The horse nuzzled him fondly, and somehow the day seemed to blaze brighter. The air was suddenly scattered with glimmers of rainbows and, in that moment, they saw what was truly standing before them: a unicorn

Elodie and Kit froze.

The unicorn's coat seemed darker than the deepest deep of the ocean. Its mane and tail were not blackest black, but a dark iridescence, like the feathers of a magpie, rippling with emerald, azure and midnight blue.

Like a night rainbow. Or a moonbow, thought Elodie.

But it was the creature's horn that stole their breath away. Transparent as rain, yet strangely luminous, it looked as if it could cut through the fabric of the world.

Elodie was speechless. The beauty and surreal, heart-soaring wonder of seeing a unicorn in the park on a Thursday morning before school felt like a moment out of time. As if the three of them had skated into a dream. Caleb stepped back, and at once the glare of sunlight faded, and the proud, fearsome unicorn became a horse once more.

"That horn," Kit breathed. "It was like looking at lightning."

"It was . . . magic," was all Elodie could manage. "We've found magic. . . It must be the last unicorn."

"Or the first one maybe?" pondered Kit. "You know, like those tropical birds that emerged from the brink of extinction after centuries of absence."

Elodie nodded uncertainly.

"We need to get back to Mum and Rufus," Caleb informed them, checking his watch like this was a totally average day.

"Yes," Kit mumbled, snapping out of his stupor, not taking his eyes from the animal, who was happily munching clumps of buttercups.

"But we can't just leave her here – the storm horse."

Caleb shrugged. "I think she goes back to her den in the shadows, so no one can find her. She knows how to hide, anyway."

"We've got to get to our violin lesson," said Kit apologetically, his face still serene with amazement.

"OK," said Elodie in answer. "I'll meet you after school by the ice-cream van. I need to know everything about our 'storm horse'," she insisted as she watched them go.

In the quiet of the gentle morning, Elodie stood before the miraculous storm horse.

"Where did you come from?" she whispered, holding out a handful of dandelion clocks.

The storm horse contentedly gobbled them up, and slowly, taking her time, Elodie stroked its velvety, dark nose. It felt as soft as feathers. The storm horse paused and looked at her so directly that Elodie felt the tug of an unspoken bond.

ASTRA.

The name came to her certainly and softly, like the stirring of a memory, and Elodie knew without question that this was the horse's name.

"Hello, Astra," she beamed, and the horse whinnied brightly. "I've got to get to school, but I'll find you at twilight, right here, I promise."

As she skated away, she watched Astra for as long as she could. But soon enough Astra was gone. Vanished to somewhere safe, Elodie hoped.

Marnie-Mae was waiting impatiently by the Feather and Fern, devouring an oatmeal flapjack and tapping the stopper of her skate crossly in the dust.

"Marnie! There you are! You're never going to believe this, but Kit and Caleb and I found a—"

But Elodie found she couldn't say the word out loud, as if that would be breaking a great code of secrecy.

"A *what*?" Marnie-Mae asked hotly.

Elodie beckoned her close. "A unicorn,"

she mouthed.

"Yeah, *right.*" sighed Marnie. She gave a flick of her indigo braids and zoomed off on her skates in a huff.

"You don't *honestly* expect me to believe you?" Marnie snapped as they headed for school.

Elodie gave an exasperated shrug. "I'm telling you, Marnie, it was real. I saw it with my own eyes – Kit and Caleb did too!"

Marnie loved unicorns. Her bedroom was full of cuddly ones with glittery manes. She had a neon unicorn school bag. A pastel-coloured unicorn duvet. Unicorn slippers in hot pink. To her, unicorns were cute, loveable things. Something you got given at birthdays. Not something that galloped around the streets of London late at night.

The rest of the day passed in a slightly tense silence. As much as she wanted to, Elodie felt she couldn't mention Astra, and Marnie was annoyed that Elodie wouldn't admit it was all a silly game.

By the time they reached the ice-cream van after school, they were both in a bad mood.

Kit came zooming over as Caleb nodded at them

from the bench he was sharing with Rufus. "So, I mean this morning was . . . wow. . ." Kit said straight away. "I've been doing some research about unicorn sightings."

Marnie rolled her eyes. "Not you as well," she grumbled.

"Apparently," Kit carried on, "ages ago, in the sixteenth century, there were unicorns that roamed the grounds of the palace, right here in the park!" Kit excitedly pulled out his dad's old phone and showed them what he'd discovered. "The evidence is taken from sketches found in Princess Grace's notebook," he explained.

They all *roughly* knew the story of Princess Grace. She was a young princess who didn't speak, but was known throughout the kingdom as a talented artist. Her mother, Queen Alice, arranged for her to stay at the palace of crystal, so she could be surrounded by nature and inspired to paint.

"It's just a sketchbook!" moaned Marnie-Mae. "It's probably all made-up." Though she was starting to sound less certain.

Elodie was about to start arguing her point for

the millionth time, when a lady in strikingly high, needle-point stilettos, a bold red beret and film-star sunglasses stalked past them and ordered a strawberry split.

Her voice was as soft as the purr of a cat, but direct, precise and utterly Parisian.

Elodie went still, trying not to stare at her, determined not to show that she recognized her from the red car in the rain, right after she had seen the unicorn. Something about the woman made Elodie feel cold, and she shivered despite the warm day.

"Elodie!" called another voice, tender as a lullaby, and all other sounds melted away.

"Maman?" she gasped, spinning on her wheels and nearly losing her balance as she fell into the open arms of her mother, Esme Lightfoot.

She smelled of sunshine and mint and hope.

"I can't believe you're here! How? What are you doing back home? Oh, Maman, I've missed you so much!" Elodie's words tumbled out as she hugged her mother tightly.

"I wanted to surprise you," beamed Maman, covering every inch of Elodie's face with kisses.

A FINE DAY IN MAY

1500s. Gardens of the Palace of Crystal

Burning Sand Spells:
Desert unicorns
Sandy in colour, with creamy manes, shire-horse hooves and white horns.

Nightingale's Heart:
Forest unicorns
Deep chestnut-brown coats, reddish manes, mossy green hooves and amber horns.

Twilight Grace:
Mist/Rain unicorns
Grey, silver or white unicorns, with lilac manes and irises.

Juniper Blue:
Valley unicorns
Often multi-coloured, but with blue horns.

From the sketchbook of the Royal Princess Grace, aged 11, listing the different types of unicorn.

Winter's Dawn:
Snow and Ice unicorns
Entirely white with glassy horns, frost-blue manes, tails and hooves.

Surf Dancer:
Beach unicorns
Golden or pale brown, with shell-pink hooves and horns, and sea-foam manes.

Indigo River:
Water unicorns
Deepest black, indigo mane, clear, ice-like horn and hooves.

Cloud-spun Dreamer:
Mountain unicorns
White or grey, clumpy hooves, and wings!

"Have you seen Dad yet? How long are you back for?"

Her maman paused, a sadness appearing in her eyes.

"I'm here on a work trip, Elle," she explained. "So I'm not staying with you and Dad."

Elodie wobbled and her maman clasped her closer. "Why?" she uttered, her hands flying to her heart as if it might break. Elodie's maman kissed her forehead, then turned towards the towering woman in the high heels who had seemingly devoured her ice cream whole.

"This is my boss, Camille de Scelerat," Maman smiled.

"*Bonsoir,*" cooed Camille in a way that was intimidatingly elegant. She leaned abruptly forward, and took hold of Elodie's chin in her long, slim fingers, staring hard at her face.

"Does she have the Gift?" asked Camille excitedly.

Elodie frowned and withdrew as her maman placed a protective hand on her shoulder. "No, no. I assure you, she does not." Camille adjusted her beret and strolled away, immediately uninterested.

As soon as she was out of earshot, Elodie seized

her mother's hand and began dragging her towards Marnie, Kit and Caleb, who were gathered under a nearby oak tree eating swirly ice creams.

"Maman, I've got so much to tell you! I saw you last night – in Camille's car, I'm sure of it."

Elodie's maman nodded darkly and stroked Elodie's cheek.

"And I saw a horse, only it wasn't a horse. It brought about a rainstorm, then I saw it this morning with Caleb and Kit, and it's not just a horse it's a—"

But Esme put a firm hand across her daughter's lips, her eyes flickering with warning.

"I know what you saw," she said in a low, urgent voice, "but you must not speak of it. Not to anyone." She looked at each of them in turn.

"Why?" breathed Elodie, feeling deeply alarmed.

"Let's go back to the flat and I'll explain. Quickly, though; I don't have much time."

And with that, Elodie, Marnie-Mae, Kit, Caleb and Rufus left the park and hurried over the road, through the bright blue door and kicked off their skates before running up the stairs to the little flat on the second floor.

CHAPTER FIVE

THE BUREAU DE SECRETS

Elodie's hands were trembling – with nerves or anticipation, she wasn't sure. Could this really be happening? Could her beloved maman really be standing in the living room, about to tell them all about unicorns?

Elodie felt as if the sky were cracking open – the way it did last night in the storm. As if a universe of possibilities was revealing itself, and nothing was quite the same.

"There's only one thing we know for sure," whispered Kit. "This is the most bizarre Thursday *ever.*"

They all settled down in the cosy living room. Kit texted his mum, Sophia, who was doing a yoga class in the park, just to let her know where they were. Not that it would be a problem. Elodie's flat was one of Kit and Caleb's favourite places and they often came here after school. Caleb adored the touch of the velveteen curtains and had cleverly positioned himself in the corner, between Rufus and the long window, so he could feel their plush softness.

Kit sank on to a beanbag. Elodie and Marnie-Mae perched at opposite ends of the sofa, still not quite talking, whilst Maman paced, glancing anxiously, her brown eyes darting every which way.

After a moment or two, Maman stilled, then began to gently speak.

"For as long as there have been dreams and thunder, there have been unicorns."

The living room fell into a soft hush, as if Elodie's maman had cast a spell. Even Marnie seemed enchanted.

"Long ago, in a different time, a terrible tempest swept through the lands, and nine fearless children found themselves stranded, with nothing to protect them but their horses."

Kit subtly grabbed his notebook from his pocket and started jotting things down. After his findings this morning, he knew that he wanted to document unicorn history.

"When the terrible storm struck, a wishing star fell from the clouds, splintering into nine gleaming pieces."

"One for each of the children," Caleb murmured to Rufus, who gave a low growl of agreement.

"Every child wished that their horse would not be harmed. And the star made their hopes real. The storm horses were marked for ever with horns of bone and starlight."

"You called it a storm horse, Elle!" Kit yelped excitedly. "This morning! You knew its name!" Marnie rolled her eyes and Caleb fiddled with the velveteen curtain.

Elodie nodded dreamily. "Her real name is Astra. I'm sure it is."

Elodie's Maman opened her eyes widely. "She communicated that to you – in a dream?"

"No, this morning in the park," Elodie explained.

"That's a wonderful thing, my love. . ." Esme said with a smile, but Elodie thought she saw something else – was it worry? – flit across Maman's face. Her maman cleared her throat and resumed the telling of the story.

"Many, many years ago, people realized how extraordinary the properties of a unicorn's horn were. Sadly, humans began hunting them across every land, until none were safe. Being nocturnal, the unicorns went into hiding, appearing in their true form only at night."

"You mean they live here? In South London? Like an owl or something?" asked Marnie-Mae, feeling utterly bewildered and a bit cross about the entire conversation.

Elodie's maman chuckled fondly.

"In a sense, Marnie, yes. They tend to stick to unknown places – highlands, deserted woodland, empty, wintery beaches – and they live all over the world. But each summer, herds – or *glories* as they are known – migrate to warmer or cooler landscapes, and occasionally a unicorn can get separated from its glory. That's when things get dangerous."

"What do you mean *dangerous*?" Elodie asked, her heart juddering.

"Unicorn hunters are still in existence, my love,"

Maman sighed.

"People want to have them as exotic pets, like tigers and crocodiles and stuff?" asked Marnie.

"I'm sure there are some circuses that would love a unicorn," answered Elodie's maman. "But it's more to do with their horns."

"Like the ivory trade," Caleb hissed, looking extremely angry.

"Very similar to the ivory trade." Maman nodded. "A horn can be used for many things: cloud cutting, curing sickness. It can be sprinkled over soup to make you look younger; its powder can heal any scar, and, if mixed with nettle and lemon balm and sipped during a full moon, it's even said to reveal the future..."

"So Astra is being hunted?" Elodie gasped, her head spinning as she remembered the car in the rain, the towering heels of Camille de Scelerat, and that strange magnifying glass... But Camille was her mum's boss. Maman couldn't possibly be hunting Astra...

Her maman's voice cut through Elodie's panicked thoughts. "The good news is that not everyone can see them. The few rare people – mostly children – who do still have the Gift are known as Unicorn Seekers. You, my darling Elodie, come from a long line of seekers, dating as far back as your great-grandmother Elyse de Lyon, and probably further."

Elodie stood up quite suddenly, her feet sinking into the sunflower rug.

"Why are you only telling me this now?" she uttered.

"I hoped I wouldn't have to tell you at all. I hoped that by not telling you, you might not discover your gift and I could keep you out of harm."

"Out of harm from what?" chorused everyone in a single chiming voice.

"The harm caused by the Bureau de Secrets. Or, as they are known in the wider world, the Society of Unicorn Killers."

Elodie fell back on to the sofa in cold, hard shock. "But Maman, that's who *you* work for... I don't understand." A million thoughts and questions swirled through Elodie's mind, making everything feel cloudy and peculiar.

Esme sank to her knees and gripped her daughter's hands.

"Yes, I do work for them – because they found me and forced me to join them – but it's not what it seems, Elle. I'm only there as a spy, to try to prevent them from realizing their plans."

Everyone in the room gazed at Elodie's maman blankly. Then Marnie's face lit up brighter than starlight.

"Oh. Double. *Wow.* You're a secret agent! Your mum's a secret agent, Elle. That's *properly* awesome."

"Are you?" Elodie whispered.

"Of sorts. . ." Maman answered. "Now, there isn't much time. Astra is in a great amount of danger and I'm going to need all of you to lead her to safety while I try to throw Camille off her scent."

"Of course!" they all cried, gazing at Esme in a state of wonder and excitement.

Then the room whirled into a hive of activity. Caleb pointed out on a map the exact location of the Rainbow Gate and where they'd sighted the unicorn that morning.

Elodie and Kit tried to draw Astra, so Elodie's maman could guess which one of the nine glories she belonged to and work out where she had been headed when she got separated.

Maman's guess was that Astra was an Indigo River unicorn. A water-based unicorn that was most likely travelling north, towards Scotland or even Norway.

"We could take Astra back to Scotland in Dad's coffee van!" Elodie cried excitedly.

Her maman glanced at her a little doubtfully.

"You could, my love. If we can tempt Astra out of the park."

"Caleb's very good with her, I bet he could do it," Elodie exclaimed.

Esme grinned a little uneasily. "All right then. But let's wait until twilight."

They all stared at each other with wild, fluttering hope.

"Twilight," they whispered, before running down the stairs and pulling on their skates and heading back to the park to pretend that this was a perfectly normal Thursday evening, just like any other.

CHAPTER SIX

YOU CAN'T TAME A UNICORN

Twilight fell across South London, turning the air the colour of mist and scattering the lake with the twinkle of stars. The park slipped into an eerie silence. The dinosaur statues were still and sombre.

The Feather and Fern had closed early. The joggers and dogwalkers had all headed home. Even the green parakeets were still, peering brightly from the treetops.

Elodie, Kit, Caleb and Marnie-Mae – all in their roller skates – waited in a crowded bundle in the shadows of an overgrown blackberry bush near the Rainbow Gate. Time seemed to tick by slower than the turning of the seasons, and Elodie felt jittery.

Marnie-Mae was trying very hard to manage her impatience. She wasn't entirely sure what to expect – was this unicorn even real? If it was, she was *definitely* getting a selfie with it! Kit was cool and calm. As someone who loved science, he was used to the natural pace of things and knew that great discoveries couldn't be rushed. Caleb was having a splendid time. He just wished the others wouldn't all breathe so loudly. He didn't mind them being here, it's just he would have preferred it to be him and Rufus and the city stars.

As the new moon glimmered far above them, there was a stirring of dust and a shift in the air. The unicorn stepped out of the fading light. They all spontaneously gasped, for there is nothing more magical than seeing a creature of myth and legend standing proudly before you.

Astra shook her moonbow mane, which shone deep greens and flashes of dark azure. When she moved into the soft gleam of summer moonlight, Elodie and Caleb could see the lethal glare of her crystalline horn, like a shard of black ice. And though Marnie and Kit couldn't quite make it out, their eyes were stung with the glow of it, like the moment after a firework lights the sky.

"Now," whispered Kit, as Astra padded inquisitively towards them.

Caleb moved confidently out of the shadows, his hand outstretched, holding the last bite of his blueberry muffin from that morning. Astra whinnied affectionately and took a small prancing step towards him. Elodie held her breath. It was *working* – the unicorn trusted them. But then she felt the air turn icy cold and heard the distant – but swift – click and clack of high heels hurrying towards them.

Elodie shot out of the shadows, startling Caleb and Astra, who backed away.

"It's not safe," she breathed, placing her hands on Astra's soft nose and sending a thought straight from her heart to the unicorn's own, mouthing the word at the same time.

"*Run!*"

In a cloud of mist and gravel, Astra bolted, vanishing out of sight. Elodie spun on her wheels, seized Caleb and Rufus and tried to haul them back into the shadows.

"What did you do that for?" Caleb snapped, pulling away from Elodie's touch and gazing forlornly after Astra.

"*The hunters are coming,*" Elodie pleaded. "We've got to hide!"

"OK, but no one breathe in my ear," said Caleb, trying to lead Rufus into the bush. But Rufus refused to move, curling up instead on the ground.

"He'll be fine," whispered Kit, but he looked nervous as the four of them hid in the spiky blackberry bush. The click and clack grew louder and louder, and a woman in stilettos and a blood-red beret strutted furiously towards them.

Camille de Scelerat.

In the blackberry-scented darkness, the four friends held hands. Elodie squeezed her eyes closed.

Camille de Scelerat hardly noticed Rufus, other than to step over him in a long stride. Instead, she marched up and down, peering this way and that, before pausing at last and taking the oddly large magnifying glass from her pocket so that she could examine the ground.

She's found Astra's prints, thought Elodie, her heart sinking.

Camille glanced up sharply, as if she had sensed Elodie's very thought. But instead of approaching the bush, she strutted away, muttering in French under her breath.

When at last she was gone, the entire blackberry bush seemed to breathe a heavy sigh of relief as the four friends tumbled out of it and scrambled gratefully to their feet.

"That was terrifying!" breathed Marnie-Mae. "That wicked lady your mum works for is *properly* scary!" Elodie glanced around, but of course Astra was nowhere to be seen. They had missed their chance to protect her... Astra was still in danger.

"Don't worry, we can try again tomorrow. We'll lead Astra to safety – I promise," said Marnie, putting a firm arm around Elodie's shoulders.

"I guess you'll have to do it without us, then," Kit said regretfully, as they skated back towards the lake with Caleb and Rufus following at their own casual pace.

"Why?"

"We're going to Spain tomorrow for a homeschool trip. We won't be back for two weeks."

Elodie's face fell.

"Do you *have* to go?" asked Marnie.

"Yes," answered Caleb, who had caught them up. "We've already been waiting eight months and two weeks. It's going to be the best trip ever!"

"I'll give you my dad's number and you can message me on your dad's phone," said Kit. "You've got to let us know what happens!"

Elodie nodded and tried to smile, but as she said goodbye to her three best friends and headed for home, a deep sense of worry trembled in her heart.

She was still wide awake at midnight, curled sleeplessly in her bed, staring out of the open window at the stars. Every so often she would murmur to herself, "Please be all right, Astra," as if saying a prayer to the moon.

At last, Elodie closed her eyes, and it was then – just as she was drifting off to sleep – that a sound reached her. A sound like something just beyond her world. Elodie bolted upright, listening to the whisper of the night wind and call of the city foxes.

There it was.

She was sure of it. It was faint, but real: the pounding hooves of a midnight unicorn galloping through the dark. Without thinking, Elodie flew out of bed and rushed out of the flat door, running down the stairs two at a time and terrifying a sleeping Pirate, who was curled up on the bottom step.

"Sorry, Pirate," Elodie whispered, before throwing open the bright blue door and letting the light of the moon rush in. There, in the moon's luminous glow, stood a unicorn, as wild as the midsummer night.

"Astra," Elodie breathed.

Somewhere close by, the wheels of a car screeched, making Elodie's heart race even faster as she stepped back and let the unicorn come to her, nuzzling her face and sniffing at her hair. She gasped with relief as Astra trotted lightly through the blue door and up the stairs, past Pirate, who hissed in horror and fled.

As quickly as she could, Elodie closed the bright blue door and crept after Astra, trying to avoid the creaky stairs. At the third step, the Singh's door swung open and eighty-six-year-old Grandma Singh frowned into the darkness.

"Elodie Lightfoot, is that a unicorn on the stairs?"

"Erm," Elodie began, "this is a—"

"Well, well, I've not seen one since I was a girl. How delightful," sighed Mrs Singh, gazing up the stairs after Astra and then smiling to herself as she closed the door.

There was no time for Elodie to be startled. She had to hide Astra.

The only room in the flat that didn't have tall, airy windows was the bathroom. Remembering that Astra was an Indigo River – a water unicorn – Elodie instinctively filled the bath, hoping that the water would calm Astra. But while Elodie was in the bathroom, Astra padded around the flat, knocked over a vase of tulips that spilled across the sunflower rug, sent the flamingo lampshade in Elodie's room into a spin, and munched on the mixture for tomorrow's blueberry muffins. Beyond the gentle chaos, Astra brought a sense of the wild into the flat, like the scent of the forest before it snows or the song of a tropical bird. Elodie knew at that moment that unicorns could never be tamed. They were made of something *other.* Something wild and timeless and uniquely wonderful. They weren't made to be caged or controlled.

Elodie sat down on the sofa and spoke to Astra in a low voice, taking care not to wake her dad. "Astra, listen to me. I need to hide you in the bathroom." But Astra only brayed in discontentment. Elodie considered what Caleb might do. She walked back to the bathroom and climbed into the cool, half-full bath – polka-dot dressing gown and all. Astra peered into the bathroom curiously. As she slowly moved towards the bath, the reflection of her horn made the water glow like liquid marble. Elodie drew back as Astra dipped her graceful head to look into the water, as if she saw something in there that Elodie didn't, and Elodie had just enough time to reach over and squeeze the door closed before the lights of a car flashed around the room and a muttered conversation in French started to float up and in through the window. Elodie held her breath.

Astra raised her head abruptly, her horn neatly slicing off part of the shower curtain. The bathwater suddenly felt freezing and, as Elodie watched, the unicorn's horn began to faintly gleam, swirling with different colours like an aurora.

There was a brisk knock on the front door, and, eventually, Elodie heard her dad stumble sleepily downstairs to answer it.

Elodie just caught his confused voice saying, "No, everyone's asleep." Lucky he didn't know Astra was hiding in the bathroom – he sounded utterly convincing.

She heard Maman's apologetic voice murmuring to her dad. Then there came the click of a door closing and the loud sound of the car as it drove away.

Elodie sat in frozen silence, listening to her dad

make his way upstairs.

"In here, Dad," she called a little anxiously.

Her dad almost fell over in amazement the moment he opened the bathroom door. It is, after all, a mightily unexpected sight to see your beloved daughter in the bath with a unicorn.

"What…? How…?" her dad stammered, before he shrugged and said, "I guess we'll be going to Scotland tomorrow then," as he helped Elodie out of the bath.

She kissed his cheek, took a purple towel and began to carefully dry Astra, who was now stretched out on their sunflower rug. Her coat was so soft it almost felt like long, sleek feathers.

"What adventures will you lead us on?" Elodie whispered as she snuggled up on the sofa. Astra gazed at her with eyes as enchanting as the first-ever stars. Elodie knew she'd go to the ends of the earth to keep Astra safe. Elodie was a Unicorn Seeker. Protecting unicorns had become her destiny.

CHAPTER SEVEN

ESCAPE AT SUNRISE

At six minutes to sunrise, before dawn had even crept across the London sky, Elodie and her dad tiptoed over the dewy grass of the park, with Astra trotting beside them. Careful not to be seen by any early-morning joggers, they led the unicorn through the back doors of the Feather and Fern. In the night, Elodie's dad had made dozens of trips back and forth from the leafy park to their flat, emptying the van of boxes, baskets, recyclable coffee cups – almost everything. The only things remaining were the coffee machine and smoothie blender.

Elodie was amazed at how spacious it now seemed, even with a life-sized unicorn in there with them. There was even room for her precious skates! As her dad loaded up the last of their suitcases, Joni and Marnie-Mae came dashing up to them.

"What's the emergency, Max?" asked Joni, still looking as pristine as if she'd had hours to get ready.

Elodie's dad lowered his voice. "We've got to leave for a few days – we're, er, working a festival in Edinburgh. So we won't be able to have Marnie, I'm afraid. Not for the next week or so."

Joni looked utterly aghast. But Marnie-Mae, who would usually have been thoroughly disappointed, had a glint of mischief in her eye. She eased forward on her skates, peering through the van's back doors and giving a little wave of joy to Elodie and a now-dozing Astra.

"You did it!" she mouthed to Elodie in sheer delight.

"There's no one else who can have Marnie while I'm working. . ." sighed Joni, her forehead creasing with worry. "After-school clubs are all full and Grandma Joss has already headed to Jamaica for the summer. I just can't take any more time off work. . ."

Elodie and Marnie locked eyes, their faces bright with hope, both thinking the same glorious thought at the same moment.

"Marnie can come with us!" Elodie yelped, trying not to startle the sleeping Astra as she leaned out of the van.

Joni bit her lip. "I don't know. . ." she breathed.

"It's fine with me," shrugged Elodie's dad.

"Please, Mum, please!" Marnie begged.

"And it's just for a week?" Joni asked. Marnie closed her eyes and gritted her teeth so as not to die of suspense.

"Well . . . OK." Joni surrendered finally, although she didn't look very pleased about it. "But she hasn't got any clothes with her."

"She can share mine!" Elodie practically shouted. She was bursting with excitement – Marnie was coming with them! They both inwardly squealed, then Elodie found herself reaching for her jacket. She was suddenly feeling cold. Beside her Astra had woken up, her horn beginning to glow faintly, like a star at twilight.

Elodie frowned. Then she shivered and understood. It was a warning. Astra could sense danger.

"We have to go now!" she cried, hauling Marnie-Mae into the van.

"Bye-bye, I love you," called Joni, leaning in to plant a lipstick-coloured kiss on Marnie's cheek and frowning at Astra before Elodie's dad closed the van doors, hopped into the driver's seat and revved the engine.

With that, the green van that looked like a floral work of art was rattling its way out of the park, circling the ring roads of London and heading for the north of England and on towards Scotland.

Only Joni saw the cherry-red car that pulled up in the park moments after the van had left, and the elegant woman who climbed out. Joni very much admired her shoes, and she might have asked where they were from, only something in the woman's expression made Joni stop, and she headed for her train instead.

In the back of the van, Elodie and Marnie-Mae stared at each other in whirling excitement. They had never been on a trip together – except with school. All their childhoods, they had been planning an epic adventure, and now it was really happening!

"This unicorn is truly magic," breathed Marnie as Elodie reached around Astra's neck so the two friends could hold hands. Astra seemed quite content to be snuggled between them. And as the van hurtled along the motorway and away from danger, all three of them drifted into a deep and dreaming sleep.

Elodie's dream was made of night – a thick indigo, empty of stars. Through the inky darkness, she saw Astra standing upon the highest peak of a ghostly white cliff that overlooked the sea. Astra raised her beautiful horn to the moon and then she leapt, seemingly into thin air. In the dream, Elodie called out in fear, but Astra did not fall. Somehow she rose, her silhouette vanishing into the starless dark.

When Elodie woke, her mouth felt dry and there was an achy crick in her neck. She had tilted forwards in her sleep, so her cheek was resting upon Astra's back. It felt soft, but brittle like the spines of many feathers.

"I had a really strange dream and you were in it!" chattered Marnie-Mae, who was wide awake and munching a gluten-free croissant.

"Where are we, Dad?" Elodie called, too sleepy to question the coincidence. Glancing at the moon dial clock, which she'd wedged upon a shelf next to the coffee maker, she saw it was the afternoon.

"Well, girls," her dad said brightly. "The roads were practically empty, so . . . we're in Scotland!"

Elodie climbed carefully over Astra and gazed out of the back window to see the rugged, rolling hills. The air seemed full of a wonderful brightness, like sea-light.

"It's beautiful," she sighed, as they neared a small, sparkling city that appeared to have been cut into a hillside. Everywhere she gazed she saw glorious views.

"Is this Edinburgh?" asked Marnie.

"It sure is," answered Elodie's dad, as he pulled up on a cobbled street that led down to a grand-looking church. "I'll park up here and you girls can take Astra for a walk."

Elodie and Marnie grabbed each other's hands

and stepped into a day as fresh as dawn, a mythical creature trotting at their heels.

The bonnie folk of Edinburgh were quite used to festivals and performers, and seemed to think nothing of two children and a majestic horse prancing through the cobblestone streets. Elodie felt blissfully happy, but every so often she would feel that familiar icy coldness creep over her and she'd shudder, wondering how far behind them Camille might be. Had Maman managed to distract her for long enough? But then Astra would nuzzle her shoulder and the cold would slip away. As if the unicorn knew. As if she was reassuring her.

"Dad, how does Maman know so much about unicorns?" asked Elodie as they settled down beside the Feather and Fern for a picnic of smoothies and sourdough, with Astra happily grazing on nettles and heather beside them.

"There is a book," her dad said in a low, secretive tone. "A collection of diaries and drawings and studies that lists every unicorn discovery throughout history."

Marnie-Mae leaned in. "Like an encyclopaedia?"

Elodie's dad chuckled. "More like a spell book about unicorn lore. It tells you *everything* about them – where they roam, what they eat, what their particular talents are, where to find them. . ."

"So where can we buy the book from?" asked Marnie enthusiastically.

"You can't," said Elodie's dad sadly. "It once belonged to the Ministry of Mythical Protectors."

"The what?" asked Elodie.

Her dad took a deep breath. "An allegiance of people sworn to protect unicorns. That's who your mum *really* works for."

Elodie blinked in surprise. So Marnie-Mae had been right. Her mum *was* a secret agent.

"So where's the book now?" asked Marnie, looking confused.

"It was stolen and fell into the hands of the Bureau de Secrets."

"And that's how that wicked lady knows how to track unicorns?" Marnie scowled.

Elodie's dad nodded grimly. "The three things you need to catch a unicorn are: the book, a seeker – one with the gift of Unicorn Sight – and a net made of lightning."

Elodie's face fell. "Do they have a net?"

Max frowned a little. "I'm not sure."

"We have to get Astra back to her glory before they catch up to us," said Elodie, rising suddenly.

"But how will we know how to find them? Like, where do unicorns hang out?" Marnie asked.

Elodie's dad pulled a small, scribbled-on napkin from his pocket, where an inky map had been marked.

"Your mother pushed this into my hand last night," he explained as the two girls crowded round to see. Astra trotted over too, her eyes alert and a strand of heather dangling from her mouth.

The map seemed to mark a jagged clifftop, surrounded by sweeping fields.

"This is the place. Slightly north of here. When twilight falls, this is where we'll find Astra's glory."

The Highlands, 1916
To my beloved Anushka
A study of the northern Indigo River.

Dearest darling Anushka,

How often I think of you when the pearl moon lights the waves of the sea. It is thoughts of your sweet face that keep me going. It is for you alone that, these three nights past – sometime between midnight and the breaking dawn – I set out to see if I might find the herd of the Indigo River and return your precious Emerald Star to her family.

It was foolish of me to capture her in the first place. I see that now. But it is only through your love and kindness that I have come to understand that all creatures have a right to freedom, especially a beast of such exceptional grace as Emerald Star.

You will be delighted to learn that I came across the herd – or glory as I believe it is known – as if by luck, or destiny, at the foot of the pale cliff beyond the village of Bracken Brae.

So fierce were they, such a fury they made with their dazzling hooves, that I thought myself in the jungles of Africa being pursued by wild elephants.

Emerald Star ran from me the moment she became aware of them. And they galloped to her with such proud love. It was extremely moving. So entranced was I that I camped nearby and studied them further. In doing so, I discovered something quite wonderful. Your girl is different from the others.

All Indigo Rivers have coats as dark as a raven and manes of deepest indigo that glimmer with rich iridescence. Their hooves are clear, as if cut from crystal or sea glass, and they have horns that remain translucent. But Emerald Star, as we know, has a horn that emits a deep emerald glow.

The others are able to summon the sea, creating great waves and twisting currents. But Emerald can call upon the rain, as if *drawing storms down from the sky with her will. Our Emerald loves water, as they all do, and she can swim for great distances beneath the surface without needing air. And sometimes, though I cannot prove it, she seems to run over the water as if it can bear her weight. Perhaps it just seems that way in the dark.*

Or perhaps our Emerald isn't a northern Indigo River. Maybe she has traits of the southern glory who roam all the way from the canals of Holland to Antarctica? Or maybe she is a mix of something entirely new—

CHAPTER EIGHT

SEARCH FOR THE INDIGO RIVER

The afternoon passed in a whirr of cobbled streets and fields full of mauve flowers. Clouds of gnats hung in the air as the Feather and Fern coffee van wound its way into the weathered, craggy countryside in search of the village of Bracken Brae.

Elodie and Marnie were both quiet, their eyes flitting between the unicorn and the scribbled napkin, which Elodie clutched as if it were a talisman that might guard them from harm. Astra was wide-eyed and attentive, her ears pushed back like a listening wolf, her horn completely invisible. Eventually, the van clattered to a stop in what appeared to be the absolute middle of nowhere. "Does anyone even live here? Is there any wifi?" asked Marnie as they climbed out into fields of wind-bent grasses and dancing dandelion clocks. The light was fading fast, the sky already darkening. Soon it would be dusk. And they seemed to have stopped at a crossroads.

Elodie's dad laughed. "I'm not sure about wifi, and I don't know exactly where we're supposed to go from here. We need a sign. . ."

They glanced around them, and Elodie consulted the napkin. It looked very much like they needed to be near a cliff edge.

"Which direction is the sea?" she asked, thinking of her dream.

As if in answer, Astra strode splendidly out of the van, gave a braying call that made them all jump, then began to trot at a gentle pace through one of the fields, her horn ever-so-softly glinting.

"What's going on? Do we follow her?" asked Marnie.

"Yes, we should. She wants us to," answered Elodie, feeling certain.

Max locked the van and they hurried after Astra as the last rays of sun turned the world gold, then the day slipped away into twilight.

Elodie and Marnie both felt the temperature drop

and turned to each other, laughing nervously. Even Elodie's dad shivered a little in the dusky greyness.

"Let's hope she knows where she's going," he muttered, as the field ended and they found themselves tracking into a thin stretch of trees.

"A sign!" cried Marnie suddenly, pointing at a gnarled old apple tree. Someone had scraped the words *Bracken-Brae* into its bark with an arrow pointing away from the woodland. Beneath the arrow, some other words had been badly scribed.

"*The witch's hut,*" said Elodie quietly. "Let's hope we don't end up *there.*"

On through the shadowy trees they crept, a whispering hush drawing in around them, broken only by the flutter of evening moths and the swoop of a hunting owl. Then Elodie heard another sound. Or, rather, she *felt* it: the wild cantering of midnight horses, mixed with the pounding waves of the sea.

"We're near," she gasped, as Astra reared up suddenly, more alive than they'd ever seen her. Her horn shone vibrant turquoise, her hooves gleamed every colour of the ocean. She bolted away from them, breaking the treeline and galloping out on to an open grassland that ended in a sheer, bone-white cliff. Beneath it was a beach of silver sand and the rushing waves of a stormy sea.

"This is it!" cried Elodie, her hands flying to her heart as they ran, panting and stumbling, to catch up with her. But Astra was already strides ahead. "This is where she leaves us. I saw it in my dream."

The clouds rolled away and moonlight lanced off the surface of the sea. The pounding got louder and louder until Elodie thought she might rattle apart. She closed her eyes, but Marnie grabbed her hand, and her dad threw his arm around her. "Look,"

gasped Marnie-Mae. "They're here. Its Astra's glory."

Elodie opened her eyes.

Below on the beach, outrunning wind and weather and time itself, was a pack of fearsome unicorns with the grace of storms and starlight. At the sound of them, Astra charged forwards at such hurtling speed it was breathtaking.

"She's going to jump off the cliff!" shouted Elodie's dad in alarm.

"It's all right, Dad, she'll be OK," Elodie called, fighting back tears. The drop was hauntingly steep.

"Remember, she's a water unicorn. She'll leap into the sea. She'll be OK. . ." But her voice trailed

off and she found she couldn't dare to look. Faster and faster Astra raced, matching her pace to the wild glory that was tearing along the beach, kicking sand into the air like a cloud of magic. Then she was leaping, striding, gliding into the night air with the beauty and pose of a dancer.

Elodie dropped to her knees, unable to hold herself up any longer. Her dad skidded to a halt just ahead. Even Marnie-Mae covered her eyes, but peeked through her fingers. Everyone held their breath, waiting for the sound of their unicorn hitting the waves.

But all that came was the song of the rushing sea and the gallop of ceaseless hooves over sand.

Elodie felt Marnie-Mae's breath upon her cheek as she whispered, "Elle, you're not going to believe this. . ." Elodie opened a single hazelnut eye and her heart almost slipped from her chest.

Silhouetted against the swirling Scottish sky, glittering like a freshwater pearl, was Astra, with her ebony coat and indigo mane and two huge, raven-coloured wings, carrying her across the heavens.

It was beyond magic, and yet somehow Elodie had

known this would happen. "Astra," she breathed, making herself stand. "You can *fly*."

Astra soared towards the moon, half running past the stars, half bending the night with her wings. The glory on the beach thundered on, in and out of the surf, calling to her in their wild voices, but she seemed apart from them, alone in her own starry wilderness.

"I guess she's not an Indigo River after all..." Elodie's dad murmured as they watched their unicorn fly. "So where on earth does she belong?"

"Why has she never shown us her wings before?" Marnie marvelled, spellbound. For, though Marnie couldn't always make out the unicorn's horn, the huge black wings were unmissable. Like a magpie's but even more enchanting.

Elodie's dad rubbed his forehead. "What do we do? We wanted to find her glory, but this isn't it. And we can't just leave her here – it's not safe. We'll have to get her back to the van."

Elodie sighed and shook her head. "She's nocturnal, Dad. I don't think she'll come down for hours. We'll have to come back for her at sunrise."

Thunder rocked the world and rain swept down so swiftly they all darted back towards the trees.

It was dreadfully dark in the woods, and without the light of the moon it was nearly impossible to know where they were going. After an eternity of brambles and damp darkness, they found themselves in an open field. But there was no sign of the Feather and Fern. Instead, in front of them was a little wooden cabin, an unlit lantern swinging in its porch.

"The witch's hut," breathed Elodie, with a terrible sense of foreboding.

"Let's hope she's in, 'cause I'm starving," Marnie joked, but Elodie could see that her best friend was a little frightened too.

"Fine," Max sighed after a time. "We might as well knock on the door."

Together, Elodie and Marnie approached the dark little hut. Holding hands, they knocked. The door creaked open, revealing a sparsely furnished den, decorated with flameless candles and houseplants. And in the centre of the room, wide-eyed and curious, sat a hardy-faced old woman smoking a pipe.

She raised an eyebrow at them, cleared her throat and spoke in a gravelly voice.

"Well, well. You're here at last. Do come in. I've been expecting you."

The three of them stared at each other nervously, hovering on the cusp between warmth and the storm.

But Elodie was so cold, so worried for her precious Astra, and here was a mysterious woman who had somehow been expecting them. It seemed like an impossible coincidence ... and this was clearly a night for impossible happenings. Elodie smiled and stepped inside.

CHAPTER NINE
A SEEKER'S WISDOM

"It's not vegan, I'm afraid," Morag – or indeed the witch, as she was affectionately known in the village of Bracken-Brae – said apologetically to Elodie's dad, as she ladled out bowls of steaming broth. Max gave a friendly chuckle and took a big sip anyway. They all sat in the semi-dark, around a smokeless fire that burned with a low blue flame, drinking the lovely Scotch broth as Morag filled them in on what she knew.

"So, as I was saying," Morag continued. "Twice a year, at the turn of the season, the glory passes through. In summer they head to the north and the cooler seas. In winter they prefer the waterways of Amsterdam or Venice, or the beaches of Britain and France."

"But how did you know about *us*... Are you psychic?" asked Marnie-Mae eagerly.

Morag cackled. "Gracious me, no! But when the glory comes, so do the vivid dreams. Often it's just memories or messages, except this one was quite detailed – different. And you were all in it. It was a warning."

"What does that mean?" asked Elodie cautiously.

"Your unicorn is special. Unusual somehow. She'll need protecting."

"Yeah, you got that bit right! She can fly!" cried Marnie.

"That is *most* unexpected. I had thought there was only one glory who flew – the Cloud-spun Dreamers . I've seen the occasional one pass over here, but they mostly live in the mountains."

"Should we take Astra to them?" asked Elodie's dad, looking increasingly baffled by this talk of flying unicorns.

Morag considered this for a moment. "It may be the best option, but I'm not sure it's right. There was a great Celtic storyteller named Aide of the Green Hills, who lived in these meadows in the last century," she said, staring into the blue flames of the fire. "He fell in love with a Russian ballet dancer, Anushka, and supposedly captured a unicorn for her. Anushka was aghast and told Aide she would only marry him if he returned the unicorn to its glory. Sadly, Aide died during the expedition – trampled to death, I believe – and so Anushka married his brother instead!"

Marnie-Mae burst out laughing. Elodie frowned at her, but soon found she was smiling too. It *was* a *little* funny, after all.

"Just before he died, Aide discovered something most intriguing. He found that his unicorn was slightly different to the others. She didn't bond with the pack, and in the end, she left them and walked her own path through the world."

Elodie rubbed her eyes. She was suddenly feeling very tired. "But where did she go? What does any of this mean?"

Morag shrugged. "Maybe the unicorns that get separated from their glories aren't lost. Maybe they are simply headed somewhere else?"

"So, we should just follow Astra?" asked Marnie.

Morag gave a long sigh. "Ordinarily I would say just turn her over to the night. But this is no ordinary occasion. Someone else is chasing that unicorn, and she's on her way here as we speak. Why else do you think I'm sitting here like an old fool in the dark!"

"It's Camille de Scelerat, isn't it?" uttered Elodie, as a cold shiver ran over her skin.

Morag nodded gravely. "You must take your unicorn and *go*."

"But she's in the sky! Like an angel, but also a horse, a bit like a Pegasus, but a unicorn," began Marnie-Mae.

"What she means is," put in Elodie's dad gently, "how do we call her down from the clouds?"

"Well," said Morag, looking straight at Elodie, "you must use your unicorn whistle, of course."

Elodie stared blankly. So Morag took a small, pink, sharp-edged shell from around her neck and handed it to her. "You'll learn how to do it on your own, but for now use this – it'll call her to you."

They thanked Morag and hurried back out into the

summery storm, this time armed with a torch, and raced back to the clifftop.

At first no one could see Astra, and Elodie felt a terrible panic close in, but when lightning flashed above them, they saw her dancing wildly through the violet skies, cantering straight through thunder, her wings beating across the moon in a feathery silhouette.

"She's *magnificent*," said Elodie's dad, as Elodie put the shell to her lips and blew into it like a flute. It made a sound like the wind, only higher and sweeter. A sound that seemed to ring through every galaxy. A sound like a lullaby. And with a stirring of rain and a last roll of thunder, Astra came hurtling down towards them.

"Get out of the way!" Elodie's dad yelled, grabbing both girls and pulling them to safety as Astra's hooves hit the ground at such speed that small whirls of dark smoke trailed behind her. She galloped straight past them and back into the swaying trees, so the three of them had to run with all they had just to keep up.

After some huffing and puffing, they found her by the Feather and Fern, chewing dandelions quite contentedly. Her wings were folded in against her back, invisible once more. Elodie ran so fast towards Astra she felt as if she herself might fly. As the heart-stoppingly powerful unicorn lowered her neck into Elodie's arms, warmth spread through Elodie like an internal summer.

"We have to go," she said softly, and they clambered into the van. "We need to go now, Dad! *Anywhere.* It doesn't matter, but we have to move."

Somewhere in the distance, the lights of a lone car began snaking their way through the rugged hills. In the back of the van, Astra's horn glittered fiercely.

"Got it," said Elodie's dad, keeping the van lights off as they drove away, off towards the nearest ferry port.

Barcelona Museum of Enchanted Art

Unicorn study: from the collection of Madame Mariposa

Study 10: "A Dual Glory". A unicorn of mixed heritage, which is its own unique creation. A New Star, so to speak!

The picture below is one of these such beings. It was drawn by the piano prodigy Elyse de Lyon, and is a depiction of the unicorn which gave its life for her when she fell into a lake.

I am yet to see such a creature myself, though I have been lucky to glimpse some of our Spanish glories. The bond between the seeker and the New Star is said to be incredibly special. I live in hope!

CHAPTER TEN
MOONLIGHT ON WATER

The night rolled by in flashes of lightning and thunder, but inside the luminous green coffee van all was well and everyone was dry. Elodie stared out of the rain-blurred window at the endless swirling dark.

"Where are we going, though?" Marnie-Mae asked quietly. Elodie shrugged. She had no clue.

"Why don't we text Kit to see if he's got any ideas? He's already found out loads about unicorns – he might know something else."

Elodie smiled at Marnie over Astra's poised head and fished out her dad's phone from his jacket pocket.

Hey Kit. Guess what???

Astra is NOT an Indigo River.

She is possibly a Cloud-spun Dreamer. Not sure?
We need help! Any Ideas?
PS She can fly!!

The phone pinged as the message was sent.

"We must be near civilization if you've got signal!" said Marnie brightly.

And no sooner had she spoken than they were pulling up at a fishing harbour.

"Stay here, you lot," Elodie's dad advised, hopping out of the van into the rain.

They waited in the misty, breathy darkness, Astra's eyes like jewels shining in the night. She seemed so content, bathed in a glow of serenity, as if flying had answered some deep call within her. It made Elodie feel peaceful and floaty, and she let her eyes flutter gently closed.

When she opened them again the rain had stopped and bright daylight was seeping through the van's little window, the sound of circling gulls ringing through the air. "Where are we?" she asked, rubbing her sleepy eyes.

"You're not going to believe it!" garbled Marnie-Mae, who was brushing Astra's mane with Elodie's pink brush whilst the unicorn gracefully slept. "Your dad convinced some fishermen to give us a ride in exchange for all-night coffee, and now we're in *Holland*!"

Elodie blinked in amazement, then yawned and gave a huge stretch as her dad opened the back of the van. "Perfect weather for croissants!" he grinned, making Elodie chuckle as he shared out the last few cakes and pastries from the van.

"And Kit texted back," Marnie announced. "He's found something *super* interesting! Apparently, they went to an art gallery in Barcelona and discovered a Spanish ambassador who collected artwork of unicorns! They have *loads* of paintings, but one shows a unicorn that looks different to all the others. A mix of every glory. Unicorns like that were sometimes called Dual Glories or New Stars, because they were unique."

"Does Kit know the name of the painting?" asked Elodie.

Marnie quickly messaged the boys back and they waited in a munching silence for the phone to ping.

Astra gave a disgruntled snort when the message arrived.

MOONLIGHT ON WATER.

Kit had even sent a photo. It was too blurry to see properly, but they could just about make out the name.

Elodie's dad took a swig of almond coffee and googled it. "Hey! It looks like there's a copy of this painting in one of the museums in Amsterdam – Mr van den Berg's Museum of Curiosities." He checked his watch. "We could be there by early afternoon." Both Elodie and Marnie were feeling a bit cramped and crumpled, and had hoped to avoid getting back in the van so soon, but Astra was sleeping soundly, so they agreed it was best to keep moving.

"Oh, and another thing," said Elodie's dad as Elodie finally gave up trying to brush her hair. "The painting was originally made by your great-grandmother, Elyse de Lyon."

Elodie and Marnie were stunned. This was *astonishing.*

"My great grandmother painted a unicorn..."

Why had Elodie never seen a copy of the painting before? Would the unicorn look like Astra?

Elodie had so many questions, but her dad had none of the answers.

Mr van den Berg's Museum of Curiosities was not in the main square of Amsterdam with the other museums, but tucked away on the top floor of a tall, thin house with a pointed roof that overlooked a busy canal.

"It feels so good to skate again," laughed Marnie as they whizzed through the sun-warmed streets, taking in the smell of fresh pancakes and marvelling as bicycle bells jingled around them and canal boats drifted dreamily by.

Elodie was sure she could feel the glimmering presence of other unicorns nearby, hovering in the shadows. But whenever she turned to look, all she saw was the bustling streets and colourful painted tulips.

Slipping off their skates and looping the laces over their shoulders, they entered the oddly charming museum. It was awfully crowded, and some of the exhibits were rather spooky, but, eventually, Marnie located the painting, right at the very back of the room, hanging high up on the wall. Both of their mouths fell open.

"It's her. . ." Elodie breathed. "It's Astra."

"This is one of my favourite pieces!" came a high-pitched voice behind them. They turned quickly, gripping each other's hands. Standing behind a little Formica counter was a man with a huge moustache and eyes that looked almost lilac. His teeth were slightly yellowing and his name badge read *Mr van den Berg.* Elodie felt unnerved by him, but Marnie grinned and boldly asked, "Is it for sale? Or would you do an exchange for lots of organic coffee?"

The man laughed and Elodie began to shiver, even though the museum was stuffy and hot.

"I would *never* sell such a famed painting," Mr van den Berg began, leaning closer to them and half hissing. "The folklore that follows it is exquisite, for the artist who painted it almost *died*. . ."

Elodie tried not to react, but she gripped Marnie's hand a little tighter.

"Luckily, her life was spared when the very unicorn in this picture gave its own to save her."

A bead of sweat ran down Elodie's neck and she began to wobble. Beside her, Marnie took her arm.

"Do you know what happens when a magical being gives up its life for you?" the man continued. His voice was too high, too strange. "You are gifted the unicorn's horn and all of its powers, and they remain in your family for many years to come. Isn't that right, my love?"

"I believe that is indeed correct," said another voice, cutting through the chatter – smooth, low, but a little clipped and unmistakably Parisian. A tall, elegant shadow moved through the crowd, and in seconds Camille de Scelerat towered before them.

Elodie was speechless with shock.

"That *is* the truth, isn't it, Elodie?" Camille almost sang, moving closer and closer to them.

Elodie shrugged in disbelief.

"The horn is in your family and you *will* give it to me," said Camille quite pleasantly, even as she reached to grab a handful of Elodie's curls. But Marnie's hand came down on Camille's wrist in a swift, deft chop.

"Run!" Marnie cried, pushing Elodie out of the way and then leaping into the air, kicking her legs high and striking hard enough to knock Camille's beret clean off her head. She spun the other way and sent Camille tumbling over, before pirouetting superbly out of the way.

Elodie didn't need to be told twice. She charged down the stairs, her heart louder than thunder. Glancing back in desperation, she saw to her immense relief that Marnie-Mae, her best friend in all the world, was pounding down the stairs behind her.

"Come on!" Elodie screamed as they flung on their skates, grabbed each other's hands and shot through the streets of Amsterdam, skidding out of the way of bicycles and tourists, several times pulling each other back from the canal edge, until finally they reached the Feather and Fern and leapt head first into the back.

"Go, Dad, go!" Elodie shrieked as she yanked the door closed, waking Astra, who gave a rather cross whinny then settled back to sleep.

"Whoa, what?" answered her dad in alarm, starting the engine nonetheless. And then they were careening over quaint bridges, past wonderful townhouses and summery cafes, away from the city.

"You were like a *superhero*!" Elodie mouthed to Marnie-Mae. "You totally saved us!"

Marnie gave a proud flick of her wonderful hair. "I know," she beamed, giving Elodie a high-five over the top of Astra's horn.

Elodie glanced at her dad, who was still questioning them about what happened at the museum.

"Is it true about my great-grandmother?" she asked as she finally caught her breath. "Did a unicorn give its life for her? Do we have its horn? Is that what Camille wants with Maman?"

Elodie's dad gazed at her in the van mirror, his eyes wise and sad.

"I don't know, my love. The book – or manuscript – of unicorn history was given to Elyse, but stolen after she died. So I don't know much else. The Ministry of Mythical Protectors has been trying to get it back ever since. . ."

Elodie tried not to let the tears come. Everything they'd learned – it was all steeped in so much mystery. There was *so much* she still didn't have the answer to. She sighed and pulled out the little rusted jar of secret lotion that she'd hidden behind the moon dial clock, hoping the comforting scent would soothe her. The lid was jammed shut as always, and incredibly hard to open, but eventually it turned, and all at once the van was filled with the aroma of rain on a midsummer eve.

Astra opened her jewel-bright eyes, alert and searching.

Then came the rushing saltiness of the sea.

Astra shook her raven mane, its deep colours catching in the light like a moonbow.

Followed by the swift and heartbreaking sense of melting snow.

Ever so faintly, Astra's horn began to glow.

"What's going on?" asked Marnie. "And what is that smell? It's like . . . moonlight."

Elodie hurriedly closed the rusted tin and stared

in amazement at the lid. It was embossed with the silhouette of a winged horse – always had been. But Elodie had never really given it much thought. All she knew was that the lotion was "magic" and "secret" and had belonged to her great-grandmother Elyse.

But now a strange feeling came over Elodie, and she held up the tin to the light, studying it closely. Even though the rust had smudged some of it away, she could just about make out the imprint of a unicorn's horn.

She gave a small, tight gasp as her maman's words came rushing back to her.

"For a horn can be used for many things: cloud cutting, curing sickness, healing any scar." And then Elodie knew, with the certainty of rain clouds before a storm, that the story of Elyse being saved by a unicorn was true, and that this tin somehow contained an element of its horn.

Paris, late in the evening
From the will of Elyse de Lyon

To my granddaughter, Esme, and your beloved child,

As you know, being a seeker runs fiercely in our family. It has been such a great honour to know of Storm Horses. Or unicorns, as you like to call them.

As you are also aware, my life was saved by one such creature. Her name was Raven and she was an Indigo River I befriended as a young girl by Charl de Lycée. She had such a majesty about her. The adventures we had were wild imaginings made real, until she had her little foal. The foal, Midnight Wish, was unlike anything I've ever witnessed: part Indigo River, part Cloud-spun Dreamer, and yet she belonged to neither glory.

Midnight Wish eventually cut her own path through the clouds on the night of a glittering tempest in the city of Prague. I have not seen her since, but I dreamed she, or a unicorn related to her, came to find you. So keep your heart open and eyes bright – as I know you will.

I have made three paintings of Midnight Wish. One I am leaving to mon petite granddaughter, one I have entrusted to a dear friend in Spain. One I have sold to a gallery in Amsterdam. When a unicorn saves your life, you are gifted with their horn, if they so wish it. And because of this, ever since the day Raven gave her life for me, I have been pursued by the Bureau. Though I've outwitted them many times, I know they are getting closer. It will take all of your courage and wit to protect Raven's legacy and keep unicorns safe from those trying to harm them.

So I entrust to you the maps I have drawn, along with a collection of letters, notes and sketches from unicorn seekers all over the globe. I call it "The Map of Lost Unicorns". You must not let the Bureau learn of its existence. With the map is the tin of the winged horse: my beautiful Raven. Esme, you must never let this fall into the wrong hands! I know you understand the importance of this.

Lastly, I leave you with the knowledge that unicorns are more discerning and mysterious than we ever realized.

Guard this information and these possessions with your life, my darling.

All my love,
Elyse

CHAPTER ELEVEN

THE CITY OF ANGELS

Once Elodie's dad was sure they weren't being followed, he pulled up in the shade of a windmill. "The painting in the museum looked *just* like Astra," piped up Marnie-Mae excitedly. "And it was near a beautiful bridge guarded with stone angels," put in Elodie.

Her dad frowned. "That sounds like Prague."

His phone pinged, making everyone jump. Elodie checked the message and was delighted to see it was from Kit. "The painting *is* of Prague!" she yelped in amazement. "Caleb found out all about it and really wants to see it, so they're driving there. They'll be there by Tuesday."

"Maybe we should join them..." her dad said, frowning. But Marnie-Mae shook her head, her indigo beads rattling. "No way. Camille Scary-rat is bound to follow us."

"True," Elodie's dad agreed. He looked troubled. "But if there are other unicorns there like Astra, then this could be our best chance of protecting her."

"Maybe we could travel at night," Elodie suggested. "If Camille's trying to track us, she won't be expecting that."

"Isn't that when Astra's awake, though?" said Marnie.

Elodie nodded. "She can run or fly alongside us."

Everyone's eyes widened at the shared memory of Astra galloping furiously through the storm, like the astonishing beauty of a sunrise over the sea. Now that seemed impossible, but it *had* happened. As if sensing the loveliness of the memory, Astra blinked her eyes open. They gleamed like deep-sea pearls in a sleeping ocean.

"We'll travel by night," Elodie's dad agreed. "We've got to do everything we can to keep her safe."

★

At six minutes to sunset, Max started up the engine of the Feather and Fern. Elodie and Marnie-Mae had walked to the nearest little town and grabbed as many snacks as they could carry, while Astra munched on daisies beside the van.

Elodie took a long, leaf-print scarf that belonged to Maman and lightly harnessed Astra to a copper calla lily on the side of the van. Very slowly, Max began to drive with Astra trotting superbly alongside, the two girls hanging out of the open coffee hatch, their hearts wild with the rush of the rich summer night.

"To anyone watching, we just look like a coffee van being steered by a horse!" whispered Marnie bursting out laughing.

"I think we look a little stranger than that." Elodie grinned. And even though they were travelling so slowly, with the wind in their hair and the stars bright above them, their unicorn cantering alongside the van, the two friends both felt that this was the most wonderful night adventure they'd ever been on.

Any time Elodie felt a sharpness of cold – or Astra's horn gleamed – Max pulled over, into fields and hedgerows or the shelter of softly swaying trees, until the danger seemed to pass.

And that was how they did it – roaming the land by the light of the moon, night after night, town after town, city after city, country after country, through rain and starlight and the rising dawn. Until on Tuesday, at six minutes past sunrise, they trundled and trotted triumphantly into a city of stone bridges and carved angels, arriving in a huge town square with an ornate mechanical clock.

"We're here!" said Elodie's dad, stepping out of the van and having a big stretch. "We're in Prague!" He peered merrily at the sky. "And it's perfect weather for croissants." The sound of wheeled skates rolling over stone made Elodie turn, and she gave a scream of joy as Kit, Caleb and a very hot-looking Rufus came charging towards them, nearly knocking all three of them over.

"You're here!" yelled Caleb as he lovingly threw his arms around Astra, who was chewing thistles, still tethered to the van.

"We sure are," grinned Marnie, high-fiving Kit.

"I can't believe she can fl—"

"Shhhhh," said Elodie nervously, glancing about.

"We need to go somewhere quiet to talk. And we need to find the bridge from the painting."

The four friends left Caleb and Kit's mum and Elodie's dad enjoying an oat milk coffee, with Astra sound asleep in the back of the van, and set out to explore the stunning city of Prague. The day was already bustling with early morning tourists, and it was easy for Elodie to feel swept along with the crowd as if this were a regular holiday; as if they were four friends just skating around a beautiful new landscape. But every so often she felt a spike of cold and ducked into the shadows along with her friends.

"So Camille knows you've got Astra and she knows your mum's lied about you being a seeker?" asked Kit when they'd found a quiet spot near an old palace nestled upon a hill. Elodie nodded.

"But she doesn't know Astra can fly," she added cautiously.

"Are you sure?" asked Kit. "I mean, the painting *Moonlight on Water* looks exactly like Astra."

"No, that was another unicorn painted by Elle's great-grandmother Elyse," Marnie explained. "That unicorn gave up her life for Elyse. And Camille reckons Elle's got the unicorn's horn, like, hidden under the bath or something."

"And *do* you?" asked Caleb very seriously. Elodie shook her head, not quite telling the truth.

They skated on, thrilled by the rough and smooth turns of the sloping city. The cobbled roads made them bounce, spin and laugh. They might have been a challenge for less-skilled skaters – but not for these four brilliant friends. Everywhere Elodie looked she was entranced by statuesque beauty. And, just as the mechanical clock with its curious dancing folk chimed three, they came across a bridge of stone as white as marble, lined with statues of heaven-sent angels, their wings open to the sky. "This is it," sang their four voices, as if they were one.

"It's *definitely* the bridge from my great-grandmother's painting," Elodie murmured. "This is where Astra might find her glory."

They explored and examined every inch of the bridge, but beyond its angelic grandeur there was nothing spectacular about it. Even the clouds above it were pleasant and stormless.

"We'll have to come back at twilight," sighed Marnie as they skated back to the square, ready to splash in fountains, marvel at the sweeping sights and laugh so much that Elodie could almost pretend this was a perfectly normal summer's afternoon.

CHAPTER TWELVE
MOONLIGHT ON WATER

Night fell across Prague, and the city glittered as though it were enchanted. Lanterns flickered, streetlights shimmered, stars twinkled, and beneath the statue of a singing angel on the far side of the bridge, a cellist began to sweetly play. Music spilled through the evening while people chattered happily and wandered over the bridge.

Elodie was nervous. Beneath the outstretched wings of an angel, she gripped Marnie-Mae's hand, laying her other against Astra's soft feather-strong back. The unicorn's body was poised, and her eyes burned with such clarity it was unnerving. None of the passers-by seemed too interested in the beautiful black horse. Its wildness seemed to keep them away. Nor did anyone give much thought to the boy curled up at the foot of the bridge with a huge dozing dog.

They were on the opposite side to the cellist, but the melody still moved them.

"What happens now?" asked Kit, who was trying to perfect his backwards crossovers.

"I guess we wait to see if other unicorns appear," whispered Marnie.

Elodie nodded. "Or we follow Astra if she runs."

But Astra *didn't* run or lead them anywhere. Instead, she trotted quite peacefully back and forth over the bridge, coming to a rest beneath various stone angels. So they waited, and the moon rose higher and higher, lancing down its silvery light like a gateway to another world. Eventually, they all sat down with Caleb and began to play cards. The music seemed to spin a gentle spell over them, making their worries melt away. As if all that mattered was that they were together.

But on the seventh round of lucky sevens, Elodie felt it. The biting cold that seeped into her skin. Then came the click and clack of odiously high shoes. Rufus gave a low growl, and Elodie leapt to her feet, spinning around on her skates to give a sharp gasp.

The bridge had somehow emptied of people. It was completely deserted, except for the cellist on the far side who continued to play. Astra lingered close to Elodie, her horn every colour of the northern lights: beautiful, ethereal, but brutally sharp. Near the centre of the bridge, in a beret the shade of blood, stood Camille de Scelerat and a hollow-faced Maman.

"It seems you were mistaken, Esme. Your daughter does have the Gift after all," breathed Camille in a tone smooth as cream. Maman pressed her lips together but said nothing. Camille gave a playful sigh that reminded Elodie of a cat sharpening its claws.

"Now come here, Elodie Lightfoot, and we will do an exchange."

Elodie didn't move. She was aware of Kit and Marnie-Mae rising up on either side of her, as if they were about to take off in an arrow formation: her two friends like her two wings. Marnie-Mae made a menacing face and, though Elodie couldn't swear it, she thought she saw Camille draw back ever so slightly.

"She's bound your mum's hands," whispered Kit urgently, and Elodie saw it was true. Maman's hands were tied together with something that looked like a band of silk, but flickered and flashed.

"Is it a ribbon of lightning?" hissed Marnie-Mae. "Like the net they use to trap unicorns?"

And Elodie understood then, at the same time as Camille spoke it: "We will swap your mother for your unicorn."

Elodie tried to swallow down the panic as Kit and Marnie both gasped in alarm. Her thoughts raced, but one rose to the surface. Something wasn't making sense. "Why isn't Astra running?" she murmured under her breath. Every other time Camille had shown up, Astra had bolted or melted into the night. Yet here she was, as calm and compliant as the snoring Rufus.

Caleb glanced up from where he was still seated, arranging the cards. "It's the music, I expect. It's making me very sleepy."

Elodie turned to gaze at the cellist. He looked ordinary, but his peaked cap was covering most of his face. "We've got to stop him," whispered Kit.

"It's very simple," Camille continued, peering acutely through her huge magnifying glass at Astra. "You lead the unicorn to us. And you can have your Maman back."

Maman gave a subtle but sharp shake of her head: *No.*

"Or I will simply take them both," Camille chuckled.

"You can't have the unicorn," said Elodie coolly. "She doesn't belong to you. She doesn't belong to *anyone*. She's as wild as the night and the wind and the stars, and I won't let you hurt her."

Camille rolled her eyes and snapped her fingers impatiently. The tempo of the music picked up and, to Elodie and her friends' horror, Astra began to pick her way daintily across the bridge.

Marnie nudged Elodie roughly. "Your shell whistle – use it!"

Elodie's hand was shaking as she pulled it from her pocket, but she blew into the pink shell with all her might, and a keening, high-pitched note rang out like a bell. Astra immediately stopped and reared up, shaking her mane in agitation, but she still seemed tethered by the melody of the cellist's music.

Camille tapped the toe of her pointed shoe with annoyance. "We're wasting time here – and your childish tricks don't stand a chance." But Elodie blew the whistle again. And this time there was a wolfish growl as a huge, wet, hairy dog came careening out of nowhere, barrelling straight into the cellist and knocking him to the ground.

"Yes, Rufus!" cheered Kit in amazement. No one had noticed Caleb and Rufus slink off and creep through the river to the other side of the bridge.

Now Caleb shot forwards and grabbed the cellist's bow out of the man's hands. "You are a bad person and your music is dull," he declared.

"Get up, Magnus!" Camille hissed and the cello player leapt to his feet.

The shell whistle trilled a third time. Camille gave a hot shriek of fury as Astra pounded across the bridge towards Elodie. Then Camille was flinging something that crackled and fizzed into the air.

"The lightning net!" Elodie screamed, as it fell with a burning flash over Astra *and* Rufus, capturing both animals in a web of storm-spun power. Astra charged at the net with her horn, and for a moment the structure wobbled, as if Astra were conducting it, the lightning sparking off her horn. But the moment it touched her cheek or muzzle, she backed away in fright, clearly hurt.

"No..." Elodie gasped, skating towards the unicorn.

"No!" shrieked Marnie, shooting forwards to fight.

"No!" bellowed Kit, flying after Marnie on his skates.

"No," said Caleb, very sternly indeed, and he held out the cello bow in front of him like a sword, marched up to Camille and knocked her beret off her head and straight into the hands of a praying angel. Camille swore very loudly in French, but could do nothing as she was still holding the ribbon of lightning that bound Esme.

"Let my dog go *right now*!" Caleb demanded.

"Don't be *ridiculous*," she half-spat at him, and that was when Caleb noticed the book protruding from the pocket of her dramatically long rain mac. And he decided in that moment to do something very brave.

"I'm very sorry about your beautiful hat," he said in a slightly forced voice, "but I just need my dog back. Please!"

"No," hissed Camille swatting him away as if he were a fly. Caleb grabbed the precious book from her pocket and hurled it into the river.

Camille shrieked as if she'd been bitten by a shark.

Esme gasped in utter dismay. Elodie and Marnie both cried out, realizing what the book was at the same time: the treasured document of unicorn lore.

Caleb skated boldly towards the net, an unnoticed smile playing upon his lips.

"Caleb, come away – the net will harm you!" called Maman in a desperate voice. But it was too late. Caleb struck the net with the cello bow as if it were merely cobwebs. The net sizzled and spluttered, the bow caught fire and, quite suddenly, the entire thing shifted its energy to engulf Caleb too. Caleb ran to his dog's side, not caring about the danger he was in.

"My brother!" Kit roared, but Marnie-Mae grabbed him and pulled him back. "It's lightning, Kit. It's not safe for any of us."

Elodie stared at the ribbon of lightning around Maman's wrist. It twisted like an electric eel, holding her fast, but it didn't seem to be hurting her.

Why?

Then Elodie remembered about the power gifted to whomever a unicorn gave its life for. How it could be passed down generations. She pulled her velvet scrunchie out of her hair, letting the night wind dance through her curls. She hoped it would be enough. Taking a deep breath, she shook out her hair and walked towards the net. As she drew closer, she could feel its heat and danger.

Astra's eyes, fierce with sincerity and longed-for freedom, met Elodie's.

I'm coming, said Elodie with her mind. *Hold still.*

Around Elodie, her friends called out, but she hardly heard them. Her focus narrowed until all that existed was Astra. She remembered Caleb on the first morning they had seen Astra, the way her horn had become visible when he had leaned against her. *She responds to love.*

I love you, thought Elodie with all her might, and the unicorn took a step towards her. Elodie held out her hands, feeling the scorch of the net. Astra's horn glowed fearsomely and, as the two of them reached each other, Elodie took a deep breath and reached into the fibres of the lightning net, letting it come to her. Her hair flew up around her, and her heart filled with love for her unicorn.

Esme gave a petrified scream. Marnie-Mae started

to cover her eyes but couldn't help looking. Kit squinted with anguish. Caleb hugged Rufus close.

Lightning hissed and the net flickered and shook as every strand of crackling light found a tendril of Elodie's hair, and as she twirled on her skates, she became a girl of storms and fire, with the net rising around her in a halo of lightning.

Thunder tore at the air, the sky suddenly full of rain, and Astra reared up, braying furiously. The net broke, swirling like a tornado of blue energy back towards the sky.

Then everything happened at once:

Camille began yelling in wild fury.

Esme broke free and ran towards her daughter.

The cello player leapt to his feet and tried to stop her.

And above them all, the sky cracked open, and there, churning up the clouds with the beat of powerful hooves, was another winged unicorn, startlingly similar to Astra but with a mane the shade of ancient gold.

Somehow Elodie knew what would happen next. And though she knew it was right, it hurt her.

Closing her heart to the pain, she let Astra go.

I love you. Now go, she called with her mind. Astra spread her graceful wings, huge and regal and deep as the night.

But as the unicorn took a step forwards, Camille reached her, eyes burning with fury and the ribbon of lightning still in her hands. With a snarl, Camille hurled herself on to Astra's back, trying to harness her. Elodie gritted her teeth and shook out her curls. Little sparks of lightning still raged from the ends of them, striking a pale, rain-washed statue of a weeping angel, making it wobble then crash to the floor, its stone wing catching Camille and knocking her over.

"Go," Elodie breathed.

And Astra leapt from the bridge, tearing through the storm, her wings spinning the stars and beating a rhythm of freedom and heart-soaring love as she rose heroically into the sky, a legend come real.

There was a rumble, and the entire bridge trembled. The clouds above churned and the sky became a swirling, ceaseless darkness that swallowed every star. Then, almost as quickly, it cleared and the night settled to a peaceful indigo, as if nothing at all had even happened.

Elodie fell to her knees. The midnight unicorn was gone. The lightning had disappeared and Elodie found herself crying.

Then Maman was whispering in her ear, soft and reassuring, and Elodie let the scent of sunshine and mint engulf her. Marnie-Mae reached out for her hand, Kit helped her up and Caleb – for the first time in their lives – hugged her while Rufus licked her scraped knee.

Camille and the cellist were long gone. But so was Astra, and nothing could stop the ache in Elodie's heart. Maman embraced her. "It's over now, Elle. You did it. You saved Astra and you freed me."

Then her maman turned to Caleb and ever-so tenderly stroked his cheek. "You were very brave, Caleb – Rufus is lucky to have you. Although, the book you threw in the river is actually very important. It was stolen from my mother years ago. But it's better that we lose it completely rather than it being back in Camille's hands."

For a minute Caleb looked confused, but then he said simply, "I didn't throw the book in the river."

"What?" said Kit in disbelief.

"Yeah – what?!" echoed Marnie-Mae.

"I didn't throw the book in the river," repeated Caleb. "I just pretended. I threw my toffee apple in the river and hid the book under my jumper as I turned." And as everyone watched, he pulled the book from beneath his jumper.

Kit, Caleb, Marnie-Mae and Elodie all laughed. Even Rufus barked in delight.

"What you did with your hair was so clever," Maman said, running her fingers fondly through Elodie's curls. "You were like a girl made of storms."

"Yeah, how did you do it? How did you know the lightning wouldn't hurt you?" Marnie asked as they headed back through the moonlit streets towards the Feather and Fern.

"I didn't know for certain," Elodie said quietly. "But I've got this rusted tin of hair lotion." Here she gazed at Maman, who lovingly cupped her face in her hands.

"Oh, Elle, that's just some old rosehip balm I got in Paris," she said, giving Elodie a sly but unmissable wink.

"Anyway, when I realized that unicorns' horns are crafted from lightning, I knew I had to try to draw that lightning away from. . ." But here her voice trailed off. The sorrow of saying goodbye to Astra was still too raw for her to manage. She wouldn't see Astra again, maybe ever. Tomorrow they would start the long drive home. Maman would come with them – no more Bureau for her. And even though this was all Elodie had ever wanted for as long as she could remember, she still felt a terrible ache.

She climbed into the back of the van – her rainbow-laced skates still on her feet – and curled up in the space where Astra usually slept. Breathing in the scent of moondust and rain, Elodie closed her eyes, letting sleep come and dreams wash over her.

Marnie-Mae laid a blanket over Elodie, and Kit, Rufus and Caleb climbed in beside her, as if keeping watch, so it was only them who noticed the little electric blue bolts of lightning still glimmering defiantly in Elodie's hair.

In Elodie's dreams came the pounding of unstoppable hooves as a unicorn the colour of midnight raced towards her. Elodie found herself standing upon the highest peak of a mountain, her hair drawing lightning out of the sky, clearing the clouds so Astra could reach her. Then they were together, and Elodie felt herself lifted by strong, gracious wings. Wings that could carry her across the world.

When the dream ended and Elodie opened her eyes, she found she was holding a single dark, iridescent feather. Like a magpie's, only sleeker and longer. A feather from a unicorn's wing.

CHAPTER THIRTEEN

DAWN OVER LONDON

At six minutes to sunrise in the vast city of London, where the sky can turn from brightest blue to gold-tinged grey in the blink of a dreamer's eye, Elodie Lightfoot gazed out across her lovely leafy park – as she did every morning – searching the long shadows for a glimpse of movement.

The sound of Maman singing in the kitchen floated down the hall with the scent of Parfum de Rose, and Elodie smiled. She squeezed her spiralling ringlets into a bun, trying not to feel too shocked at the tiny darts of blue light that still sometimes fizzed through her hair. But Elodie only loved it all the more and never used the "magic lotion" now.

"Six minutes till we leave, Dad. You almost ready?" Elodie called.

They set off together now, all three of them, and Maman planted a playful kiss on Elodie's dad's cheek and mockingly said, "It's perfect weather for croissants." Elodie felt warmth in her chest, and she beamed as they walked through the park, with its green parakeets and greying autumn sky.

At the sound of wheels whizzing over tarmac, Elodie pulled on her rainbow-laced skates and flew over to her best friend in all of South London, sweeping Marnie-Mae into a tight hug. Her braids were deep turquoise now, and her skates were new, but her firm belief in unicorns was undeniable. As they circled each other in a backwards dance, Kit came tearing towards them, tracked by Caleb and an even slower Rufus.

They high-fived and sat down together to pore over Kit's notebook. He had decided on the journey home that they would update the book of unicorn lore, adding all they knew. It was – part secret heritage, part guidebook, part map – for anyone else who should ever stumble across a unicorn. They had already added everything they'd learned from Astra, Morag and even Camille, including their recent discovery about the power of music over water unicorns.

"So, we know loads about Indigo Rivers, and a bit about Cloud-spun Dreamers," Marnie said, "but I reckon if we started a vlog about it, more people would come forward with information."

"We're not starting a vlog," Elodie laughed as they glided back towards the dinosaurs.

She loved this time of morning when all the dreams for the day felt possible. The boating lake was every colour of autumn, dew sparkled upon tiny wildflowers and, in the soft early light, if she looked at the statues hard enough, Elodie could almost imagine they were real.

"It might be a good idea to go global though, eventually," said Kit.

"Some things are best kept secret" smiled Elodie, and behind her Caleb silently nodded.

For a moment, Elodie stumbled as she skated – she was sure she'd seen something whiter than snow move through the trees. She glanced behind her, but there was nothing except the swaying branches, the lake and the misty London skies.

As the others skated on, Caleb dropped a chunk of blueberry muffin on the leaf-layered ground. The park was still fairly empty, so no one noticed a white horse of striking elegance emerge from a thicket of wild asters. Its hooves were closer to crystal than bone, its mane was the blue of winter rivers and, when the autumn clouds shifted in the sky, Caleb could make out a dagger-sharp horn, clear as glass.

He smiled to himself and wandered dreamily on.

The Feather and Fern Coffee Van
South of the Misty River

London, sometime in Autumn

How To Be A Unicorn Seeker

Dear Reader,

Hey! We hope you're having an excellent day, because its about to get even better, bigger and brighter. Let's begin by telling you the story of how we discovered a unicorn in a South London park at twilight. And not just any unicorn . . . a Dual Glory – or a New Star! A creature the colour of midnight, with a lightning horn and magnificent wings.

She was extraordinary, and magical, and heartbreakingly beautiful. And more than anything, she was our friend.

One of the first, or last of her kind, Astra was being hunted by the Bureau de Secrets.

Through a series of fortunate adventures, we were able to protect her until she reached her glory, and her life was saved.

Now she is somewhere on the other side of thunder, and we are eating gluten-free croissants and missing her. A lot!

So we have sworn allegiance to each other to keep a look out for unicorns and guard them from harm.

These are some of the impossibly possible things we learned along the way, that could help you become a Unicorn Seeker too:

1) A unicorn can appear at anytime: in dreams, at the edge of a lake at dusk, or below your bedroom window on a rainy Tuesday evening. Always be ready and never doubt yourself if you see one.
2) Unicorns move freely among us and stay hidden by appearing to be horses. People who recognize them straight away are official Unicorn Seekers. Being a seeker is a very lovely gift, which is sometimes passed down

through families or can just occur naturally. Anyone can see a unicorn if the weather is right. (Hint: look for a mild storm.)

3) If you want to make friends with a unicorn, always carry a gluten-free muffin, dandelions or thistles, and drop crumbs or petals on the ground. Stand very still at twilight. And listen with your heart – you will feel the unicorn's presence more than see it.
4) Remember they are *WILD* and cannot be tamed. They adore moonlight, and respond to LOVE. So always be welcoming and respectful.
5) All unicorns are different. Some love water, some live for snow, and others need sunshine. Use this book to help you identify the different glories and discover what your unicorn delights in.
6) If you do lots of seeking and still never see a unicorn, that's OK. Unicorns have to remain secret. So don't worry at all, just trust that they are there, and they appreciate you thinking of them.
7) Lastly, if you do find a unicorn and you're

worried for its safety, please write to us at the above address.

Yours faithfully,
Elodie, Caleb, Marnie-Mae and Kit.
AKA, The Unicorn Seekers of South London.

ABOUT THE AUTHOR

Cerrie Burnell is an author, actor and ambassador best known for her work on CBeebies, a role which has earned her critical recognition and a devoted fan base. During her time on CBeebies, she has broken down barriers, challenged stereotypes and overcome discrimination to become one of the most visible disabled presenters on kids TV.

Cerrie is the author of twelve children's books including *Snowflakes*, which she adapted for the stage with the Oxford Playhouse in 2016 and the *Harper* series, which includes a book that was a World Book Day title in 2016. She has also created a one woman show, *The Magical Playroom*, which premiered at the Edinburgh Fringe in 2013.

Since leaving CBeebies, Cerrie has appeared in the BBC continuing drama *Doctors* and made the eye-opening documentary *Silenced* for the BBC. Her newest book *I Am Not A Label* published in 2020 and was one of Amazon US's "Twenty best children's nonfiction books" of 2020 and was the overall children's choice winner of the SLA 2021 Information Book Award.

Cerrie is currently the BBC's ambassador for disability.

Photo by Lynda Kelly